PEOPLE PIECES

PEOPLE PIECES

A Collection of
Mennonite and Amish Stories

Merle Good, Editor
Allan Eitzen, Illustrator

 Herald Press, Scottdale, Pennsylvania

PEOPLE PIECES

dedicated to the memory of

ESTHER EBY GLASS

*a friend, a faithful Mennonite
Christian, and an astute writer*

Other Works by Merle Good

Books
Happy as the Grass Was Green
These People Mine

Dramas
Stranger at the Mill
Who Burned the Barn Down?
Sons Like Their Fathers
Yesterday, Today, and Forever
A Lot of Love
These People Mine
Isaac Gets a Wife
Thanksgiving May

Contents

WINDOWED MIRRORS
OF OUR LIVES

My father learned to speak English by going to school. He grew up speaking Pennsylvania Dutch, the low German dialect of many Mennonite and Amish groups. But I, his son, can neither speak nor understand the dialect. In one generation, a beautiful language has been laid to rest, and with it, a whole way of life.

This book celebrates that changing way of life. Eight other writers have contributed to this kaleiodoscope of stories about our people. None of the seventeen stories seeks to sum up all that we are — or all that our lives might mean. Each story is like a windowed mirror — reflecting, piercing, and interrogating the texture of our living. Each tells and shows a bit of the whole. Taken together, this collection seeks to bring the reader many and varied impressions of what it means to belong to a people, a community.

Belonging to a people is a sometimes mysterious experience. One does not live completely to himself in a community. Joys are shared, as are fears and sorrows. But being a people is no more static than is a big cloud in the sky. To some our subculture may appear monstrous and unchanging; but in fact it is forever revolving, interacting, and transforming while somehow hanging together: that's a people. That's us.

People Pieces does not concern itself with impressing readers about how good we are; how much we are in need of God's grace has long been apparent to both our neighbors and ourselves. Rather, this collection should be understood as an ad hoc effort by some of us who love our community, carving out windows from the walls of our lives so that others may see in. Each window has a different shape and size, pointing the reader to a certain aspect of our way of life and faith. And each window is part pane and part mirror, so that those of us trapped (voluntarily?) inside our lives may catch a glimpse of our own reflections.

To readers unfamiliar with Mennonites and Amish, let me say that we should be understood as a religious movement, born in Europe during Reformation times, lately settled down in various parts of the world as a people with traditions as strong as our faith. Many of our traditions embody our faith; many perhaps do not. But since when is it novel for faith and tradition to do battle? Readers interested in a serious in-depth reading of our history should refer to *An Introduction to Mennonite History* (Herald Press, 1967) by my friend, Cornelius J. Dyck, certainly one of the best introductions available.

We are not an army: our traditions vary a great deal and our leadership is decentralized. But numerous emphases have been cherished by most of our groups over the years, many of which are alluded to in these stories. One such emphasis is peace and nonparticipation in war; another is a strong stress on servanthood and the simple life; and a third theme among our communities underlines the belief that Jesus taught us a distinctly different way to approach the human situation.

When conditions and practices inside one's subculture are changing very fast, one can't tell sometimes if it's good or bad. Is this the death of our people — or is this the pain before new birth? Many voices rise up to interpret the meaning of the changes. We too wish to be heard; that's why we brought this collection together.

Many of these stories deal with growing up, an experience common to all humans, yet somehow unique to each of us. Other stories raise the mood of death, such as J. D. Stahl's "The Dark Behind the Door." Some of our tales explore the meaning of service and caring; "Gertie" reveals many of our inadequacies; "The Present Strength" depicts a man in a strange world, doing what he knows best; wanting to show love and not knowing quite how has long been one of my own writing themes.

Other stories center on the concern for peace and forgiveness; Ken Reed's "My Name Is Joseph" is certainly a most unusual tale, based on a true story. Several pieces, such as Levi Miller's sensitive "A Visit to the Zoo," takes a look at our own differentness. And several stories focus on the extremism lying below the quiet surface of our culture.

The windows of these people pieces will not show the reader everything inside our lives. Our goal is to add to our literature several more panes (and/or mirrors) which might help us better understand the comings and goings of our precious faith and community, our people, and our changing way of life.

This book is dedicated to the memory of Esther Eby Glass, who lived, worked, and wrote among our people here in Lancaster for many years. I am donating any royalties I receive from the sale of this book to the Esther Eby Glass Writers Award, a fund providing annual awards to young writers.

Merle Good
Lancaster, Pennsylvania
Christmas, 1973

PEOPLE PIECES

WAITING

By Sharon Hoover

SHE'D BE waiting for me even though it was past one in the morning. She had always stayed up waiting when we were out late. Mother'd be sitting in the old armchair in the kitchen, her body draped in a long baggy nightgown that fell to the floor, with her black hair all flowing down and an old tattered prayer covering on top. Oftentimes she'd be reading the Bible or studying her Sunday school lesson. And when we children would come in, she'd ask how our evening was. Where we'd been. Sometimes I didn't feel like talking and I'd just answer real shortlike and go off to bed. Those times I remember seeing her eyes turn darker and she'd look real hurt. But Mother was never one to dig.

I stared at the road ahead, past the rain slashing down

against the windshield, to the yellow line hardly visible. The windshield wipers were slapping time to the radio blues and I wished for the dry, warm safeness of the house. But thinking of coming back to Mom and Dad scared me. It'd be the first time in about seven months that I'd seen them. In fact, it'd be the first time since I left for college. I hadn't come home for Christmas because I was traveling around with a chorus at school. At least that's what I told Mom and Dad. Oh, not that it wasn't true. It's just that I could have gotten out of going if I'd really wanted to come home.

I'd changed so much since I left home and I didn't feel like trying to explain and justify everything about me to them. About the length of my dresses. Slacks. My music. My boyfriend. My politics. My God or lack of Him. Mom and Dad were all right but they'd never gone too far away from home and couldn't understand college life. Not that they didn't want to — just that they couldn't.

As I neared home the roads became more familiar and my mind glided over the landscape even though the darkness made it impossible to see. There was the old schoolhouse where Dad had gone when he was a boy. In front of it was the old pump with a green plastic cup stuck on top. Down from the schoolhouse was the Stoltzfus farm. They had a huge family, thirteen kids altogether. It seemed they had one every year I could remember. Then there was the old people's home where I used to work, cleaning. I saw the old women's faces, tired and creased like brown crumpled pastry sacks. The old men, toothless and gray, sitting on the porch smoking.

The Hellers' homestead was next, a white house and barn — our minister's place. Always as neat as a photograph. Trimmed lawn, clean windows, freshly painted buildings. I wondered what Sue would think of me now that I'd changed. Would we be able to communicate at all? She'd been my closest friend before I left. She had wanted to major in English but since her parents didn't like the idea of her going to college she decided to wait a few years.

As I moved along the road I knew each bump and slowed before crossing them. Moving faster with the familiarity of the roads, I was a homing pigeon with a weight around his leg. The weight of fear.

Then there was our lane, long and narrow, still the old dirt road it'd always been. I slowed coming in the lane, partly in an effort to dodge the ruts and partly because I was trying to gather my mind for what was inside the darkened house. As I neared the barn Shep, the collie, started to bark. He barked at everything. I used to get so mad at him I'd kick him in the head and call him bad names but it never helped much.

The door was unlocked as usual and I tiptoed inside. Mother was in her chair as usual, too. But she was sleeping. That was unusual. Mother had never fallen asleep waiting for us children as far back as I could remember. She looked so at peace with things, sitting there, her chin hanging down on her breast with her old, black tattered Bible resting in her hands. Mother looked so much older than I'd remembered. Her thick black hair was sprayed with gray and her skin was wrinkled white.

I thought perhaps it was the poor lighting that made her seem so aged. It increased my fear about how she would react to the changes in me. Slacks, she would say, are not ladylike and the Scriptures teach that a woman should not dress in men's apparel. She couldn't stand the short length of my dresses before I'd left and I knew she'd harp all the time about the ones I brought along now, even though they were the longest ones I owned. Mother would not like my short hair either. Every time we'd go somewhere and she'd see a Mennonite girl with a shag or something she'd say, "My, how that must grieve the Lord." I had a pixie.

But now sitting there asleep in the kitchen chair Mother looked so peaceful, so lovable. I felt a terrible urge to hug her but I didn't, not knowing how it was between us. Instead I decided to find something to eat. Maybe she'd get up and I wouldn't have to wake her on purpose. But she slept on, even when I dropped the knife on the floor and slammed the refrigerator door. It was funny being in the room with her sleeping. I kept feeling as if she were looking at me when I had my back turned but every time I looked she sat eyes closed, resting. I finished eating and still the only sound was the spigot dripping and rain pounding on the windows.

I guessed I'd have to waken her. I couldn't leave her sitting there till morning or she'd have a stiff neck. I touched her hand calling, "Mother, Mother, it's Laurie, it's me." She didn't respond and I pulled back petrified. I remembered feeling cold flesh only once before — at my grandfather's funeral. I was five and Mother said, "Touch his hand, Laurie." I hadn't wanted to, but I did so I wouldn't look like a fraidy cat. Mother had said, "This is the touch of death."

Suddenly sitting there in the kitchen I wanted to scream. This was all so unreal. Maybe she wasn't my mother. Maybe it was the wrong house. The wrong place. The wrong time. But I didn't scream. What could screaming do but scare me more?

I stood slowly, tiptoeing up the steep stairway to Mother and Daddy's room at the top. How could I tell him? How could I make it easy for him? Opening the door, I tiptoed into the room and awakened him. "Something happened to Mother, Dad. Come to the kitchen."

He woke. "Why, Laurie! Good to have you home, Laurie. What'd you say? Mother's in the kitchen?"

"No, Dad, Mother'd like you to come to the kitchen."

He moved first down the steps, shaking his head as he went. "What does she want at this time of the night? My, but it's good to hear your voice, Laurie."

"Well, Mother, what would you like?" he said before coming through the kitchen door. "Kind of late at night to wake a fellow up, you know." He saw her then, sitting there with her chin resting, sitting so peaceful. And he seemed to know what had happened without even touching her. He looked at me almost accusingly. "By God, by God," he whispered. And it was a prayer.

The first time I saw Sue was at the viewing and we didn't talk much. I didn't even try. It seemed everyone looked at me with dark accusations in their eyes. And I knew what they thought. Eyes tell stories. They thought I'd killed her with my wickedness. My short dresses. My not coming home. My slacks. My waywardness. I hated those eyes and I was glad when Dad and I could be left alone. But even then there were terrible silences. It seemed Dad was deep inside himself. Dad had gone with Mother.

One day I went to call Dad for supper. He was up behind the barn, staring at the pink of sunset fading away, his back toward me. Dad looked so old there, standing black against the sky. His back was stooped, his hair unkempt, his pants mud-splattered. I knew if I could see his eyes they'd be far away somewhere. It seemed they always were lately.

Standing there behind him I wanted to run up and hug him. I wanted to beat him on the chest, crying out my pain and anger, feeling that he'd understand. More than this I wished I wore long dark skirts with dark stockings and had shiny dark hair up in a bob with a prayer covering to crown it. If only I could walk up and put my arm around his waist and share these thoughts with him. But I wore a shorter dress with knee socks and had a pixie. My arms wouldn't even go around his waist.

Instead I said, "Nice sunset, isn't it?"

"Yes. Sure is," he agreed in that far-off voice. "You know your mother used to love sunsets. I remember when we were young and just started farming we'd go for walks at sunset in the summertime and she'd tell me stories about what was happening as the sunset changed and moved in the sky. She could tell such good stories. I wonder what she would have told about this one."

We were silent together. I didn't know what to say. It was as if I wasn't there to him. The silence was deep, almost eternal. And I knew it *would be* if I didn't break it. There had been too much silence between us, cutting deeper into our hurts.

"I'm sorry," I blurted. "I'm sorry. Please understand." For the first time since I'd come home, Dad turned to me, and his eyes were there, looking at mine, and he held me at arm's length looking at me. Then pulling me close he cuddled me near his heart and I remember smelling the barn in his gray flannel shirt and hearing his heart beat real steady.

"I understand," he said. "I understand." And we wept together, mixing our tears until the silence made no difference. Until the silence felt good. The sunset was gone then and we walked into the house washed and clean in the story it had told.

Sometimes I think that's all Mother was waiting for, just to rest in peace and finish her book of sunset stories.

THE TIME WE HAVE FOR LIVING

By Merle Good

I HAD THIS problem I wanted to talk to someone about. I'm not exactly sure why I went to Joe about it. Joe was never quite the kind of guy I went to with problems. But I thought perhaps he could help me this time.

I hadn't seen Joe for months. And in a way he hadn't changed a bit. Same old good-looking kid with that corny expression on his face. Only he wasn't so corny tonight. He just sat there rubbing his bloodshot eyes, chewing a piece of grass, and talking like he was fifty years old or something.

"The time we have for living is not very much," he said, "but I guess it's enough."

Man, I didn't know whether to laugh or cry. So I just breathed in with my mouth sort of halfway open like. I could not for the life of me understand what Joe was talking about. But I guess that didn't really matter. It was like I wasn't there and Joe was talking to himself. Only he was talking to me.

"You didn't know me as a football player, did you?"

"No," I said, "no, I didn't." And I didn't. Well, my goodness, in high school you couldn't have gotten Joe to even look at a football until you'd cleared out all the girls. I mean Joe had more girls waiting on him in one day than I spoke to all year. Well, that might be a little exaggerated — I didn't talk to that many girls.

"College does something to a fellow," Joe was saying.

"That's what they say."

"Oh, you wouldn't know," he said. "You've always been a married man."

I didn't say anything. What can you say?

"I had this roommate named Lester," Joe said.

"Lester?"

"Yeah, Lester."

"Well, what kind of guy was he?"

"A football player." Joe sat there thinking it over for a moment. "Yeah, that's about it. Lester was a good football player. Otherwise he was a plain dummy. That sounds unkind but I don't mean it that way. Lester was not the kind of guy who should go to college. He'd just come back from two years in Vietnam and he wasn't exactly popular around campus, if you see what I mean. He wasn't intelligent, he wasn't that good-looking, and he didn't know what he was going to major in! But football — all that guy lived for was football, football, football. You see what I mean?"

Well, I thought I did. "Ah — in other words, Joe," I said scratching my head, "in other words, this guy Lester was a football player."

"Yeah, dummy, of course. He was a football player. Not varsity or anything, but intramural. One of the best. I mean, he had a body, a real body, with muscles and everything. He was really strong. And that's okay for a while. But after a few weeks it started to get to me. I felt like I was living with a lion and I was just one hundred and sixty-eight pounds of bone and flesh. And blood. So I thought, man, I can play football too. So I up and joined one of the other teams. And it was okay. Football's a lot of fun.

"Anyhow, this one afternoon Lester's team was playing our team and, man, we were way behind. So our captain says, 'Hey, you guys, you gotta hold Lester.' And it was true, Lester was breaking through all the time. So the next play three of us hit him. Hard. We knocked him down. He stayed down. They took him to the infirmary and the infirmary took him to the hospital. But it was nothing serious, they said.

"Well, a month later and he was still in the hospital. He was much better they said, so I didn't sweat it. I'd go and see him now and then. Then suddenly one day — it was all over."

I looked at Joe. "You mean Lester died?" I said.

"Yeah, yeah." Joe was very quiet. His eyes froze in his face as he sat there staring. "I mean, I never even thought about it, man. They said he was getting better. See, I was one of the guys who hit him. I was one of the guys." Joe bit his lip.

"Well, anyhow, his girl friend Martha — see, I didn't even know he had a girl — this Martha came around to see me and told me all this stuff about Lester that I didn't know. Real exciting stuff. Apparently his family always had to struggle for a living and, in his little hometown, Lester was known as the guy to help people out in a pinch. And Martha told me about some of the close scrapes he had in Vietnam. I couldn't believe it. Man, I had no idea. All Lester ever was to me was a football player.

"So I asked Martha how come Lester had never told me any of this stuff, and she said, 'I guess he didn't know you cared.' Boy, that's really telling it. Then Martha looked at me and said, 'But you did care, didn't you?' "

Joe looked at me. "Man, what can you say? How can you live with a person and know nothing about him? See what I mean?"

I nodded as Joe continued. "But then I saw that Martha knew, 'Why is it,' she asked real quietlike, 'why is it that it's only after people are gone that we care for them?' "

After Joe had finished his story, he and I just sat there for a long time. After a bit I remembered why I had come, but I realized he wasn't interested in my problem tonight. Tonight Joe was caught up in caring for a football player who was no longer here to be cared for. So I left.

PEOPLE PIECES 3

MY NAME IS JOSEPH

By Kenneth Reed

MY PRINCESS was floating on the river with her long hair swimming backwards on the water like a shoal of small black fish. She was too good for me.

I stood under the tree on the bank and held up a sweet peach. "Ariwaha."

Instantly the water splashed and she disappeared beneath the surface. The river here is not deep, but its bottom is black. With the sun dancing on the water I couldn't see anything. No sign on the shore above, no sign on the shore below. Had she gone beyond the bend? Impossible. A fear rose and I dropped the peach and the rifle. "Ariwaha." I shouted and leaped.

She was laughing on the bank when I broke surface in the middle of the river.

"For me?" she asked, and held up the peach.

I held her at arm's length later to rebuke her. Surely that was a dangerous thing to do. But she shook her head and I felt my heart softening. How beautiful she was, the girl I would marry. Her hair was long and thick and black and her eyes were always pools whose surface changed. Now big and wondrous, now warm and smiling, now drooping with sleep, now winking wickedly with laughter. Her arm tinkled with many bracelets.

"Ariwaha," I said, and forgave her for deceiving me.

"Your clothes are wet," she said. "People will wonder if you always swim that way."

"I will tell them a tree on which I was crossing the river broke."

"They will ask why you cross the river on a tree. Why not wade across at a shallow point?"

"Then I will say I waded in to get a duck I shot — see, I did shoot one — and stepped into a hidden pool!"

"They will ask why you didn't take off your clothes to get the duck and why you are not more careful when stepping in the river."

"In that case I will say I would gladly have taken off my clothes, but the chief's daughter was swimming in the river and she is not a good enough swimmer to retrieve a duck. She almost drowned herself."

Her eyes widened with delight.

"You are too intelligent. How can I marry such an intelligent boy? I think I should choose someone more like myself, Blue Eyes."

"I dislike the name."

I wound her long hair around my arm.

"Look, it's like a snake that will not let me go," I said.

"Perhaps, I won't if you are intelligent, Todo. Come

and see how I will feast you," she said pulling my arm. "The lily roots are big and sweet this year. Are you alone?" She turned suddenly and looked out past my shoulder.

It was no small thing for a Delaware girl to be seen with a man, even the man who was to be her husband. At best, her reputation might suffer.

"Yes."

How lucky I was. My princess was comely and a dozen men as bold and sure-armed as I had spoken for her. Thirty bearskins for the princess. They lay in her father's house and the scars on my arm spoke of my valor and love for her.

"Who has ever heard of a warrior with eyes blue like the eyes of a pigeon?" they taunted me — my friends, but now my rivals.

"Thirty bearskins? The boy will be eaten alive."

"She is noble," my rivals said, "but no noble blood runs in him. No, not even Indian blood — only white blood, every drop of it. The blood of the men who are gobbling our land and hungry to kill our fathers and brothers who are Delaware."

The story is long. I have forgotten it. I only remember that my mother washed me and washed me until she had washed all of the white blood out of me. She plucked my hair until only a fistful stood up. She darkened my body with walnut hulls to make me look like her child by birth. She plastered my hair with bear grease until the red curls became black and straight. I burnt in the sun. My tongue spoke as true Delaware as any of my brothers, and in the dark when I spoke, no one could tell that I was different.

But when the sun came up, the roots of my hair shone red and my eyes were blue.

"So you will be a blue-eyed Delaware," she said, and loved me in spite of it.

It was on the long hunt north beyond the great lakes that I found at last that I was a Delaware, though as often as I looked into a hollow of still water the face didn't change. "You will grow weak and tired," my father prophesied, "but on the day that you do, the Great Bear will appear in heaven and point the way to food and safety."

The pile of bearskins in my pack grew. But the nights also grew colder, and it was time to return to my father's town. Food gave out and my feet dragged. Clouds began to fly overhead, thicker and grayer, and I feared I would be caught in snow. I fell down exhausted and piled the skins around me to keep warm. "If you see this Delaware," I said to the Spirit, "send your sign."

At midnight the clouds broke and the sky burst with stars. Low on the horizon I saw the Great Bear twinkle and beckon. I followed him to the top of the hill and into a cave. There I found wildcat kittens and ate them. It was as my father had said. The Great Spirit of the Delaware had adopted me as his true son.

"Todo." It was my princess behind me on the trail. "Perhaps you should wait here."

She was right. We were nearing the town and some woman washing her clothes might see us together.

"I will dig only the fattest roots for you," she said and slipped by me.

The trail along the river was unsafe in the summer. White hunters and occasional white soldiers sometimes found this trail and stumbled north toward the village. If they were lucky, they returned alive. If they were caught, it was the end. The Delaware had a dozen unsettled scores.

The sachem, of course, watched all of this with the wise eyes of fifty years, and I saw his growing uneasiness. Perhaps this would be the last year of the Susquehanna. Other villages were moving west rather than fight an enemy with superior weapons. We had few guns.

Perhaps that was why he watched me.

"Todo," he said, "you will be our ambassador someday. You are Delaware, but you are also white. Do not forget that." How could I when resentful young men constantly reminded me? "Someday you will take word from the Delaware to the white men in Philadelphia that we desire nothing but peace. Nothing but peace. You know our hearts, you will marry my daughter, and someday you will speak for our people."

"But how can I speak for our people when I have forgotten the white men's language? Do they have an interpreter who will tell them the meaning of my words?"

"Perhaps," said the sachem.

I recalled my childhood and I didn't want to go back.

"Perhaps you remember when you were a boy," said the sachem, quick to read people's minds.

"When I do, Great One, I quickly forget it."

"When you marry my daughter, you will be one of my family. It will be the best of two great peoples, the Delaware and the white people. Many white men are good; do not forget it."

"No," I said, but I hardly believed it.

I waited for my princess on the bank of the Susquehanna and watched evening coming from the east. Swallows winged down over the river, snapping flies above the water. I was hungry . . . even a lily root . . . I left my rifle and the duck under the leaves and went to look for her.

STRANGE voices . . . laughter . . . I run up the hill on the trail. . . . Ariwaha, Ariwaha . . . beyond the hill, where the creek bends . . . white skins . . . long black hair . . . my bride with strange men, their arms around her, pushing her down . . . my gun . . . still under the leaves . . . will they hear me? I am running up the trail, my rifle to my shoulder and . . . the white skins fall. . . .

"Joseph, put that gun down. Joseph," a voice remembered. *Joseph.*

I run down the hill to my beloved's side, and she is lying between the dead, ugly bodies, caught under one of them.

Ariwaha. My beloved is naked and torn. Her long black hair is dirty and full of leaves, her eyes . . . her eyes hold a different reflection than I have ever seen before. Great pain. But when she sees me, they grow warm and she repeats my name again and again. The light in her eyes flickers . . . and goes out. I cover her with her torn clothes and carry her gently up the creek to a dry spot. I hold her carefully against my chest and comb her long black hair and wash her wounds and touch her eyes with my lips.

Ariwaha. I bury my beloved by the creek where she dug lily roots.

The men are still there in the morning. I look at them again, their faces carved forever with hate. I hate them. They have killed my beloved.

IT WAS there by their bodies that I heard the voice again.

"Joseph, put that gun down."

Joseph? It was my name. No, not my real name, but my white name, and he had told me never to forget it. He was my father, but not my real father. My real father was an old Delaware, much respected in the town council, but this was my white father.

"Yes."

His voice seemed in the woods about me.

It is good to listen to the voices of the spirits, my Delaware father had told me. "It is good to listen because they will bring you a message from the Great Spirit who will tell you how to be wise."

Now it seemed that my white father's spirit was in the woods with me.

"Come back, Joseph," it seemed to say. "Come back to the new house by the spring and live with me, because I am well." How could that be? I had seen the Delaware capture and bind him and hold a long knife to his throat. But I did not ask the spirit. When he spoke, it was good to listen. He told me again of my childhood, which I had forgotten.

Yes, he, my white father, was a wise man who loved our people, the Delaware. When he came to Kittatinny from a far country, he built his cabin by a spring near the Blue Mountains. The spring was frequented by our people but my father was not afraid of them. He brought them into his cabin and let them sleep before the fireplace when they were on the road north in search of meat.

"They are our friends," my father told us. "One never points a gun at a friend. 'Love thy neighbour,' the good Lord says."

My mother, not my real mother, but my white mother . . . I remember her as a fat woman, always laughing, always bearing children. She was a good Amish woman, yes, and wise in the traditions of her people. She loved her children but she did not understand that this was also

Indian land and everything which grew on it belonged to all who passed through. That was the Delaware custom. She made bread and butter and gave it to the warriors whom my father invited in, but she did it grudgingly. She saved the best pieces for her family.

My father never went to sleep with his door locked.

"Open the door, boys; we are going to sleep." When we woke in the morning, sometimes a stranger would be sleeping by the fire.

But one summer, when I was twelve, the Delaware stopped coming to the cabin and neighbors began to report horrible stories of white soldiers from the east coming to push the Delaware out forever, and of battles, cabins burning, Delaware villages burning, angry white men, angry red men.

My mother grew afraid and barred the door when my father was away. An Indian party came in the evening and asked for refuge. Their bodies were painted. It was raining heavily. She refused to let them in. They asked only for bread, but she refused that too, and finally ran back inside and barred the door again. We heard noises that night. In the morning, we found our dog with his skull crushed, and my father's cattle, two of them, with their foreheads broken wide open.

My father was angry when he returned.

"Why did they do it?" he said. "I have never mistreated an Indian. Were they Indians who didn't know us?"

"No," my brother and I told him. "They were the same, but painted."

"And did they ask for anything?" asked my father. And I lied because my mother had told me not to tell Father what had happened.

Then my father gathered us all together and said, "These

are bad times but we will not forget, the Indians are our friends. We do not harm our friends. But this is harder yet, boys. 'Love your enemies, bless them that curse you, do good to them that hate you, and pray for them which despitefully use you and persecute you, that ye may be the children of your Father which is in heaven.' Those are the words of our Lord."

The next time they came it was night. The warriors stood at the edge of the clearing and shot arrows with firebrands attached onto the roof of the house. It lit. We hid in the cellar. Perhaps they would think we were gone. Fire fell around us but my father poured cider onto it until at last there was no more cider. Day was dawning. Looking out, we thought the Delaware had gone.

We crawled out the cellar window and lay in the grass. My mother, though, was fat, and she came slowly through the cellar window, the last one. The house was going behind her, and a burning splinter fell on her trapped leg.

"Jakob!" she screamed. That was my father's name.

In the peach orchard a young warrior who had fallen behind to fill his pouch with ripe peaches heard her. He whooped to alert the party.

We raised our rifles, my brother and I.

"Joseph, put that gun down," my father said.

We begged him. Quickly, before it was too late, but he shook his head and threw the guns back into the burning house. I ran away before they got to us. From my hiding place in the woods I saw them kill my brother and sister, seize my father and lash his arms together, and knife my mother. Then they took me with them.

"Joseph," my father said. "Never forget that your name is Joseph Hochstetler."

And now he was telling me again; he was walking in the woods with me repeating my name. *"Joseph, Joseph. Come home, Joseph, to your father. I am well, Joseph."*

My beloved is dead, and I cannot tell her father. "Good night, princess."

I walked eastward.

On the third day I came out of the woods at my father's clearing. As he had said, there was a new cabin. I stood at the door and a young woman whom I had never seen opened the door. "Jakob!" she screamed. I reached for my knife instinctively. Like rabbits running for cover, children seemed to come out of the grass and run toward her.

I shook my head and put back the knife. I laughed.

"Jakob!" she screamed again, almost as if I were not there. He came out of the plowed field, wearing a black hat with his white hair hanging below it. He walked slowly. Yes, it was my father.

He stood before me and reached out his hand without fear. It was his custom. He shook with every stranger he met, white or red.

"I am sorry I killed," I said in broken English, and gave him my gun. "My name is Joseph Hochstetler."

THE DARK BEHIND THE DOOR

By J. D. Stahl

THE SUN rises again today. The mailman drives up, opens the mailbox, and leaves again soon. The lights go on when I turn the switch. There is water in the tap. Our towels hang at their usual place. My feet obey my command. Gravity is still in effect.

I feel heavy, heavy.

I want to sit and stare. Not move. The silence presses the sides of my head. I want to sit and let it press. Let it press hard to hold back the tears. It isn't noon yet, but it is late. Far into the day. Endless, uncounted days lie ahead. But now there is only now. Now is enough for now.

I am twenty-four. I was twenty-four yesterday. My eyes still respond to light. Beyond the kitchen window I can see ripe fields of corn, soon ready to harvest.

My wife is dead.

We had only just begun our life together. She is dead, and our child with her. The child I will never know. A boy. My son. Together, in his coming, they died.

Two years — long enough to plan our lives, to sing and to quarrel, to make love. We — what is left of we? We was she and me. What has become of we? If she is dead, then I have died, for I am part of we.

Yesterday was the funeral. So many words were said. The air inside the church hung heavy. The benches slid sideways; the walls buckled. A touch on my arm. A chill. Words I never heard.

Once I walked in a crowd in the great city. I felt the jostling of hurrying bodies, elbows, shoulders. The steps of many feet, some moving with me, some past me. The faces always changing — dark, light, painted, grotesque, bright smiling, dancing eyebrows, stubbly jaws, sad eyes, glasses, flowing hair, a wrinkle in a fading cheek, a frown on an intent face, mischief in a boyish grin, terror in a fleeing eye — all moving, flashing, changing. I observed, defended myself, caught an eye here, followed an arresting face there. I was an outsider. I did not want to belong. I was just passing through. I knew none of them. I was a foreigner, a stranger to this shifting kaleidoscope. I was merely looking to please myself, from a distance, and I was afraid. Threatened. Until something changed.

Perhaps it was caused by a shift in the angle of the light, or a drift of music across the street, or a faint but delicious smell I stumbled into. At any rate one of those mysterious rearranging changes occurred in me, giving the world a new and lively light. Now I belonged in that crowd, just as much as any of them — the fat man with the cigar, the laughing skipping couple, the child tagging at his mother's hand. I saw a brother over there, close to me and gone again. I took delight in a smile on a pair of beautiful lips, a look of kindness and wisdom in the eyes of an old man. Joy rushed through me like a deep breath, a burst of energy. Exhilaration lay in the motion and variety, and the oneness I felt.

I was glad to be a man, and to be at that place at that time. And I thought of the Creator who made these images of Himself. Even the ugliness and the brutality and distance could not hide the image. It burst through to me, like a reflection of perfect and endless joy, and I wondered in amazement at the imagination that had spun this fantasy that was reality, the source of the light that took these shapes and lived and moved. And I was part and individual, flowing in a huge crystallizing and melting mass.

I wonder if I shall ever feel that way again. I fear not. After I realized I loved her, and had discovered her love for me, we were once separated for a time — a week, I think. I remember something new and unknown happened to the way in which I looked at people. I began to see resemblances to her in every woman's face! The way the muscles played about the girl's mouth when she smiled — that was she! The cut of a child's nose — she again! The way an old lady bent her wrist — I recognized her in that! And each thing I saw gave me a pang, the yearning to feel the touch of her bent wrist, and to kiss her smile.

I remember a time from our courtship. We took a long walk through the summer fields, breathed the fragrant air, talked of the future, our life together, tangled our fingers together, and laughed. We imagined having a child, planned days and places. Toward evening, tired and happy, we found a grassy clearing near the edge of a small woods. The late sun tinged the trees hues of orange, and the yellow grass around us and across the fields shone a reddish depth.

We lay side by side, close but not together, facing each other in silence. I felt the desire like a gentle flow to put my arms around her. As we rested in thought, a deep sadness came over us, a knowledge of eternity, premonition of death, hearing the faintest rustle of the wind in the leaves, feeling the finality of sunset. Our thoughts passed between us without words. We were one. She smiled at me through tears.

Strange, that the memory of these moments returns to me just now. I have come to silence from a dreadful confusion. In the church the air was hot. I couldn't keep my mind there, it escaped frantically. Words become a blur, I choked on stale breath. I was aware only that she was irrevocably gone, and with her our child and all our images of the future. And why? A chance physical deformity, a medical emergency, a fatality not to be avoided despite the most careful attention possible? "An extremely rare case," the doctor explained. But his efforts were of no help. And no comfort now. I am alone with the stark emptiness in me, beside me, around me.

It was good to step outside, to feel sharpness of cold wind whip around my body. The mourners at the grave leaned into the wind on the side of the hill. The cemetery is friendly in summertime, surrounded by a few dense leafy trees. Now the trees stood half-bare, separate, and random. I stared at the freshly turned earth and thought, *Who will stand around the hole they will bury each of us in?* I left the tattered group and walked up the hill alone. I offered my cheeks and forehead to the wind, felt with satisfaction the fierceness tugging my hair and slapping my cheek. I wanted the whole violence of unleashed nature to beat on me, surround me.

When I reached the top of the hill, far from the small crowd below, I screamed into the wind, released my voice in pain and fury, making sounds like a wounded animal, wrenched from inside me, without sense other than blind hurt. And then I prayed, feeling the chill streaks of tears run down my face, prayed with a cracking, crying voice. And I needed God, even as I need Him now, but then I knew and expressed my need greater than ever before.

Helplessness, sorrow, loneliness, regret — these are only words that mask the reality of death. And in face of that reality, I realized my faith. Even now, as I have control over the pain, as I expect the shock to break over me, splintering and penetrating me like vicious slivers of glass, I can hope. Between the forgotten song of illusion and the burning dirge of loss I know, though I cannot live it yet, a new beginning.

When I was a little boy, my grandmother died. I loved her dearly. My mother dressed me for the funeral and turned to the door to go. But I, not understanding more than that something great and frightening had happened, dreaded to follow her. I slipped into the corner behind the door, and pulled it wider to close me in, hidden in a small dark triangle. I stood there pressed into my shelter, trembling, not wanting to go.

The sun comes up again today. And she and he are dead. I want to sit and stare. Not more. Not leave the dark behind the door.

THE DEPARTURE

By Melvin Lehman

SHE STOPPED momentarily, frying pan in hand, listening as the bed creaked reluctantly in the room above her and the sluggish feet plodded across the floor and out to the bathroom. She had heard the sound every morning for almost as far back as she could think, but this time she listened to it carefully, remembering it. Then she turned on the burner and set the pan on the low flames. He was leaving early this morning for college, and mush and puddings were the best thing to get him started off right.

If she hadn't helped to pack the Plymouth herself last evening, she could hardly have believed he was actually leaving. It didn't seem possible that it was eleven years since Timothy had left for college and all of six years since Jonathan had gone. Eugene was just starting second grade when Timothy left. She must be getting old, she thought.

When the others left, it had somehow seemed as if Eugene would always still be there. He was the youngest, and she used to catch herself thinking of him as being with her forever. But now, finally, he was leaving for college, too. In a half hour, at the most, he would be gone.

She walked over to the refrigerator and took out the mush. Reuben had been out milking for nearly an hour and wouldn't be in for five or ten minutes yet, but she suddenly found herself wishing he were here now. He was so good to her at times like this. She had often thanked the Lord for Reuben.

A husband's love was like a gift from God — something steady, something that grew, something she could be sure of. But a son's love was different, riskier. For a mother, it was almost like falling in love with another man, knowing all along that eventually he would leave you for another woman — another woman who would wash his clothes, mend his socks, and listen to him when he needed someone to talk to.

She sliced the mush, laying the pieces out on the table beside her. Now, of course, was no time to think about it, but maybe they were wrong in letting him go to college in Ohio. She couldn't begin to count the times she and Reuben had prayed that what happened to Timothy and Jonathan in college wouldn't happen to Eugene.

It was out of the question to ask him not to go to college at all — he had his mind set on that ever since grade school. Besides, she knew plenty of other mothers who had sent their sons off to college and they had gone on to work for the church, some of them preachers and others missionaries.

Maybe it was, like Reuben had said, the college in Ohio. But they had visited it a couple of times when Timothy and Jonathan were there, and it seemed like a nice enough place. Could it be the professors? What did they teach them in college, anyway?

Eugene was just like the other two when they had left. They had all been faithful members of church and the youth fellowship. They had all accepted Christ early in high school. All of them had enjoyed reading and had liked music. Each of them had fallen in love once or twice.

But college had changed everything about them she had ever known or thought she knew. It was almost as if they weren't her own sons anymore. She had sensed the change as early as Christmas vacation of Timothy's freshman year. He had walked into the kitchen looking around as if it weren't quite the same house he'd been born and raised in. He stayed home most of the time that vacation, hardly bothering to look up his old friends — mostly just studying and playing the piano.

When they were home on vacation during their freshman and sophomore years, Timothy and Jonathan had each had heated arguments with her and Reuben about such topics as evolution, situational ethics, and the literal inspiration of the Bible. On Christmas vacation of his sophomore year, Jonathan had even expressed doubts about the Virgin Birth of Jesus Christ. Thankfully, though, he hadn't talked anymore about it after that.

With both of them, the arguments had stopped in their junior and senior years. It was as if they didn't have much to say about college by then. It seemed they thought they knew so much more than she and Reuben that there wasn't much they could really talk about. What did they teach them at college, anyway? she wondered. It

When the others left home, it had seemed as if Eugene would always be with her. He was the youngest. But now he was leaving for college. Soon he would be gone, too.

must be something she was too old to learn.

She set the table carefully, Reuben's place in the center with the Bible beside his plate, her plate and Eugene's on the sides. Finally, she placed in the center of the table the shoofly pie she had baked for the occasion yesterday afternoon.

So when everything was all said and done, were Timothy and Jonathan happy? She had thought about that question for years, and she still wasn't sure. They were better to her now than they ever had been. And they smiled when they came to visit. And they remembered her birthday every year — which was more than she could say for Reuben.

But somehow, they just didn't seem to be the same sons now that she had raised and known. It was something in the way they were silent when the subject of religion was raised, something of the distant, faraway look she caught on their faces when they picnicked out under the apple tree in the backyard on the Fourth of July.

And she could never forget that one Sunday after dinner, when Reuben had casually asked Timothy about his faith. Oh, he believed in a God, all right. But what kind of God? Reuben pressed. How on earth could he know? Timothy replied. It was hard enough just believing in Him.

Then a few minutes later, while she was doing the dishes, she had overheard Timothy say to Jonathan in the living room, "Goddamn it. Every time I come here he starts asking me about my soul." She sighed. That had hurt as much as anything ever had.

She walked to the window and lifted it up, propping it open with a clay flowerpot. The morning air was cool against her stomach, refreshing after the heat of the stove. The sun was just up, level with the horizon, singing its way across the corn tassels and through the low-lying mist still lingering by the creek in the meadow. The lawn outside looked like heaven — the slanting sun rays giving each dewdrop its brief moment of shining, irides-cent beauty until the morning sun reclaimed it for its own. It really wasn't fair at all — the work of hours of quiet night air evaporating in minutes at the onslaught of the uncompromising morning sun.

She paused when she heard the clump of feet heading back into the bedroom above her head. Eugene was going to be different, though, she knew that. Something told her college would be different with him. He didn't talk as much as Timothy and Jonathan, for one thing, and he hadn't dated as many girls as the others. That was different enough, wasn't it?

She heard the rattle of bureau drawers as he looked for the last change of underwear and socks. She smiled. After his breakup with Rachael this past summer, it was almost as if she had fallen in love with him.

Rachael was a good girl — the Hostetlers were a good family. But she knew from the beginning it wouldn't last. Of course she could never have told Eugene that. He had to find out those things for himself.

Then, after it was all over, he had come to talk to her about it, and they had gotten to know each other again — almost like old friends, reunited at last. They had spent a lot of time together during the summer — shelling lima beans and cutting corn in the cool of the summer-house. She had explained to him the things he needed to know about girls that the books on life and love never told. She told him about how girls like delicate things, and how a girl needs to feel a boy wants her to love him, but shouldn't make it look like he is trying too hard.

She told him how it was important for a boy to be himself and to be a man around a girl without being crude or rough. She could tell by the way he had listened that he understood, and she loved him for it.

But now, just like the others, he was going off to college. It was a different kind of girl he would be getting to know. Now he would confide his secrets to girls she had never known. She sighed. Whether it was the girls or what they taught him she didn't know, but if Eugene was at all like the others, a year from now she would hardly know him.

She heard the kitchen door open and looked around to see Reuben walk in. "The calf's doing fine," he said, hanging his hat on a peg by the door. "It'll pull through all right."

"Good, I was worried about her. How's the mother?"

He combed his hair mechanically in the mirror over the washbasin. "Oh, the mother's fine."

The first piece of mush sizzled in the pan. "You're still sure the Plymouth'll make it?"

She heard the splattering of water and the rich, wet sound of soapy hands. "I gave it a final check just before I came in — tires, oil, battery, water, spare tire. Everything's okay."

"Gas?"

"Full."

She paused. "Reuben, do you think Eugene really — "

She was interrupted by the clatter of feet on the staircase. Then there he was, standing before them with his overnight bag in hand, smiling — his sport shirt and pants freshly pressed.

"Good morning," he said.

"Good morning," they both replied.

There was a brief silence. "How are you this morning?" he asked, still smiling.

"Oh, as good as can be expected," Reuben said. "And yourself?"

"Real good," he said, nodding. "Real good."

"Well, sit down," she said. "Breakfast'll be ready in a minute."

He took a deep breath and looked at the stove. "Puddings and mush. My favorite!"

"I made it special for you."

He smiled and sat down. "What a beautiful morning! Incredibly beautiful. I wonder if mornings are this beautiful in Ohio."

"They should be," Reuben said. "Ohio has some good country. I heard there are a lot of real nice farms out there."

She brought the steaming platter of fried mush from the stove and set it on the table. "There we are."

"My glasses?" Reuben asked. He picked up the Bible beside his plate. "I was reminded of a verse this morning —" he glanced at Eugene, "— that I think would be appropriate for the occasion." He sifted the pages near the center of the Bible. "Yes, here we are." He cleared his throat. "Remember now thy Creator in the days of thy youth, while the evil days come not, nor the years draw nigh, when thou shalt say, I have no pleasure in them."

She watched as he finished reading the chapter. She had always liked the way he furrowed his eyebrows slightly when he read; he had never altogether adjusted to the reading glasses he had gotten five years ago this winter.

When he was finished, they prayed silently. She prayed longer than usual, and when she lifted her head, Eugene was watching her.

As they ate, the men did most of the talking. They talked about the farm, about what Ohio and college were like, and about Eugene's finances.

When they were finished, they sat silently for a moment. "Thanks for the breakfast," he said. She smiled and nodded.

He cleared his throat and took a sip of water. "Well, I guess I might as well be going. Nothing like an early start."

"Eugene, you will drive carefully, won't you?" she asked as they stood up.

He smiled. "Mother, I solemnly promise to drive more carefully on this trip than I have ever driven before."

"You'll need it," Reuben said. "The highways are terrible these days."

"And whatever you do, don't forget to write," she said, walking beside him to the door.

"Don't worry. I will."

"And don't forget," Reuben said when they got to the door, "we'll be praying for you."

He looked at them both. "Thank you. I'll pray for you, too."

He paused. "Well, good-bye, Father," he said, shaking hands.

"Good-bye, Eugene," Reuben said.

When he turned to her, her eyes fluttered the briefest second and then met his. "Good-bye, Mother," he said, and kissed her softly.

"God bless you," she said, without smiling.

He turned and left then, walking out to the barn under the old pear tree in the yard. The last summer before he went to college, eleven years ago, Timothy had built a tree house out of scrap lumber up in the tree and the three boys had practically lived there all vacation, up among the branches. They had even slept in it a few times. Once she had asked to climb up and see it for herself, but no, they said, they couldn't let her do that because she was a girl, and girls weren't allowed in their tree house.

They watched as Eugene put his overnight bag in the back seat of the Plymouth and climbed in the front door. He started the motor and let it warm up a minute. Then with a final wave and a smile, he was on his way.

She tried her best not to, but there was nothing she could do to stop it. Reuben looked down at her and then, tenderly, took her in his arms. She cried softly for awhile with the kind of tears that only a good husband understands. She had often thanked the Lord for Reuben.

PEOPLE PIECES 6

SUNDAY SCHOOL

By Eleanor Smith

THE SUNDAY morning sun struggles through the windows rowing the top of the east wall — squat, square windows streaked with last night's muddy rain. It shines on the many-sized pipes running the length of the ceiling, transforming their heavy dust to thick, glowing moss.

It shines on the objects set about the room and veils their dinginess, for a few moments at least. The chalky blackboard, precarious on its three-legged stand. The flannelgraph beside it, littered with cutouts of Moses, a burning bush, a camel, an ark, a coat of many colors, an empty tomb. The upright piano, flaking varnish. The paper lilies in the china vase with a nick in the rim. The Bible verses taped to the walls, printed in a large, careful hand, attached with Scotch tape, bought with children's weekly pennies, offered to the Sunday school, jingling in a metal cup.

It shines on the new-washed hair of the second-grade children sitting with their legs twisted around the legs of small, light green chairs.

It shines on Mrs. Kropf, on her hard, stiff body carefully and modestly encased in a cotton-rayon print, new this season. On her dull, aluminum hair fastened tightly in a net, making it look like silver for a moment.

It shines on Frankie, too, and warms him. He is timid. The room, the objects, the children, and Mrs. Kropf are all strange to him.

Now Mrs. Kropf is speaking. Her mouth is all that moves, and to Frankie she is like the mechanical lady he watched advertise floor wax at the state fair. To the other children she seems no particular way at all because she's been speaking to them for thirty-five weeks now and they don't look at her anymore.

"Let's sing the 'nine forty-five' song yet. We'll see if any more come in, although it looks like everybody's here."

The teenage girl at the piano starts to play, keeping the rhythm but missing notes here and there, and Mrs. Kropf and the children sing:

Nine forty-five, nine forty-five,
Be on time to Sunday school, nine forty-five.
Nine forty-five, nine forty-five,
Be on time for Sunday school,
Naa-aa-eene for-teee-five.

Mrs. Kropf nods to the girl, who picks up her purse and goes out, savoring her chewing gum. The children don't bother to follow her with their eyes.

"Thank you, Charlene. That was fine, children."

Mrs. Kropf draws a long and resolute breath that pushes her ribs against their stiff cotton-rayon case. She says in her most cheerful tone, "Well, children, happy Sunday morning. Aren't we glad the Lord has given us such a nice, sunshiny day to come to His house?"

The children recognize the question as one that doesn't want an answer, so they are silent. It's Frankie who is interesting to them, and they crane to examine him with their round, unsmiling eyes.

"One, two, three, four, five, six, seven, eight, *nine!*" She is counting aloud and pointing at each child to win their attention, and one by one the children turn their faces toward her.

"Yes, it looks like everybody's here today. And we have a visitor too, yet. Bert, would you like to tell us your friend's name and where he lives?"

Frankie is pulling his shoulders together and painfully enduring the ordeal, but Bert is eager and his words leap out and bounce around the room.

"This here is my cousin Frankie from Detroit and they're on their vacation and they get to go to *Disneyland.* And he's in the *fourth grade!*" He looks at his cousin with envy and admiration, but Frankie is looking at the floor, feeling too tall for the green chair.

"Well, we're glad to have you, Frankie. My name is Mrs. Kropf, and this is Brenda, and Sherril, and Nathan, and David, and Carol Ann, and Carol Jean, and Bruce."

"Now!" she announces. "It's lesson time."

Without being told, the children scoot or drag their chairs into a crooked circle that includes Mrs. Kropf. While the chairs are scraping, Mrs. Kropf looks down at the teaching manual in her lap. She can't keep from picking at the peeling cardboard cover.

"Today, boys and girls, our lesson is called 'Jesus Helps Us to Be Kind.' Let's find a verse about being kind in God's Word."

She reaches under her chair and brings out a new, mock-leather Bible, gold-stamped "EDNA KROPF" in the lower corner, and opens it to the page marked with a purple ribbon.

"Here it is." She holds the Bible in front of her, stiff-armed, moving it in a slow half-circle so that all the children can see, although they can't read the small print.

"It says, 'Be ye kind one to another.' Let's all say that together." She begins, and the children's voices follow hers.

"Good! Again!"

"BE YE KIND ONE TO ANOTHER."

"That's fine. Now I'm going to name some ways Jesus told us to be kind to each other, so let's listen closely. One way is, He told us to give to the poor and to the hungry. Also, to visit those who are sick and in prison, and to invite strangers to our homes. Now, what are some ways children today can be kind?"

A little girl speaks out immediately: "We can share our toys."

"That's right, Sherril. And what else?" Mrs, Kropf looks around at the children, her eyes glittering with the effort toward eagerness.

Sherril answers again. "We can not hit back when someone hits us."

"Yes, umm-HMMM . . . and what else, class?"

Most of the children are not listening any longer. Mrs. Kropf's glance slips down to her manual.

"Well, we can forgive those who try to hurt us or say

bad things about us, can't we? Or we can give up our turn at a game for someone who hasn't had a turn. But those things are hard to do, aren't they? We need Jesus to help us. We need to ask Him every day to help us to — "

"But can't we be kind even when Jesus doesn't help us?" Frankie said that. He is blinking hard, but looking at the teacher rather than the floor.

Mrs. Kropf is smiling.

"We do need Jesus to help and guide us, Frankie. When people don't know Jesus they do bad things, like African people who sometimes drown their babies or people of India who have more than one wife. They don't do these things because they want to be bad, but because they don't know what Jesus wants them to do. That's why we send missionaries — to *tell* them what He wants them to do."

Frankie has listened with care, and he asks another question: "But what about in this country when people don't love Jesus — and they still do kind things anyway?"

Mrs. Kropf looks at her manual even though she knows the answer isn't printed there.

"Wouldn't they be kinder still, Frankie, if they knew Jesus and acted kind because they love Him, instead of for selfish reasons?"

Frankie feels an unusual certainty and he answers rashly, knowing he may be going too far.

"Sometimes they're kinder than people who know Jesus!"

Mrs. Kropf set her face in pleasant lines; Frankie can see that she is uneasy, but he doesn't know precisely why.

"I doubt if you know anybody like that, Frankie."

"My neighbor man, Mr. Snow," Frankie says. "He's about the kindest man I ever saw. And he never goes to church. And he says 'Jesus' sometimes when he isn't even mad. But he's the kindest man I ever saw."

The children are intensely caught up in the exchange even though they don't understand. Mrs. Kropf is vaguely afraid, because she knows now that she's engaged in a strange contest with an opponent who isn't fully aware that they are in battle. From her foxhole she fires a defensive bullet.

"I don't believe you could have seen him do any real, unselfish kindness that sheds God's grace abroad."

Frankie sits in silence for a while, then tilts back his head and remembers. The softness in his voice doesn't signify retreat.

"Well, he lets us play on his grass and doesn't mind if we wear a hole in the lawn . . . and he lets us puff on his pipe sometimes, and gives us corn candy . . . and once he took a stick and chased away this yellow dog that was fighting my dog, Pedro. But the best thing is, we sit up on his back porch and he talks to us about everything in the world — like we were people, not kids — and he listens to us talk, too. Once Solly asked him if he prayed to God and he said he didn't, but it's okay if others do it, he doesn't hold that against them, he said. I guess he's about the best and nicest friend I ever had in the whole world."

Now Mrs. Kropf has stationary targets. She feels her strength return. She has rolled the manual into a thick tube and spread it flat again.

"Is it good of him to use the Lord's precious name in vain, and to teach children to smoke and to not believe in God? He might have been a good man if he had let Jesus guide and direct his life."

Frankie wavers. "Not kinder, though, because he could

not be." He senses that that is not a good answer.

Mrs. Kropf, tucking at her hair, goes on as if he hadn't spoken.

"A *good* man, with a far higher purpose in life than his own selfish needs. The high calling of serving Christ Jesus!"

Frankie doesn't answer. He is crouched in his chair, twisting his fingers. Mrs. Kropf sees that she has won. She sees that he is just a little boy, a visitor at that. It crosses her mind that if he tells his mother that the teacher was mean to him, why, it would be a little hard to explain.

"Well! Time is moving on! We'd better turn back to our lesson, hadn't we, children, or we won't be finished when the final bell rings. Now I'm going to read you our kindness story. It's about a little girl named Mary Lou."

She turns a page in her manual and begins to read. "Mary Lou jumped off her swing and ran toward the house. Mother was — "

The brittle end of her sentence snaps off. Frankie has stood up in front of his chair; he is staring at her and beyond her. The children are mute. All are caught up in Frankie's trance. Mrs. Kropf is struggling against an unreasonable terror.

Frankie's voice is low and hardly rises or falls. "You know what happened? I'll tell you something that happened. Once we were over at Mr. Snow's, see, up on his back porch talking and like that. And Mr. Snow said when he was young, in the Army, he used to could walk on his hands as long as a football field without ever touching his feet on the ground. And he said he bet he could do it yet. So we said, please do it for us. And he went out in the yard and stood right up on his hands and waving his legs to keep balanced. Then he took three little steps with his hands . . . and . . . then he fell right down on his head on the ground."

The boy's voice becomes as tense as the fists pressed into the pockets of his Sunday suit.

"We yelled at him. We said his name. But he didn't answer, so then we went and touched him and he didn't move. He was staring up — but not at us! I ran home and Mom went out and came back. And she said Mr. Snow was dead. He *is* dead, I mean . . . I think he is."

He puts up both arms to cover his face.

"She said he was dead and wouldn't ever be alive anymore. Because he was too old and he stood on his hands and he died. *That's* what happened! And that was last week. And when we get back from this trip he won't be there."

Now he puts his arms down, and sets his eyes on Mrs. Kropf. In spite of the tears there is nothing of a child in his expression. He speaks with calm viciousness.

"Well, I know I hate you. Because you don't think Mr. Snow was good. But he was good. Better than anyone and better than you. And he didn't have no Jesus to make him that way."

Frankie pushes his chair back to let himself out of the circle and sets it back in its place. He walks out without looking around.

Mrs. Kropf is fingering her manual, tearing tiny pieces off. After a minute she says, "Bert, maybe you ought to go with your cousin. Take him to your mother's class."

The children are sitting very still. Mrs. Kropf tries her usual child-addressing voice. "We're sorry Frankie's neighbor died, aren't we, class? And we forgive him for saying he hates us, because we know he was upset and didn't mean it . . . DON'T WE?" This time she waits for a response. The children nod with hesitation and one little girl says, "Yes."

Mrs. Kropf bends her head to the manual.

"Mary Lou jumped off her swing and ran toward the house. Mother was calling from the kitchen door. 'Here I come, Mother,' answered Mary Lou cheerfully. . . ."

The Sunday sun climbs in the summer sky, rises above the row of rain-barred windows in the basement room, leaving it gray. It leaves Mrs. Kropf's hair without the illusion of silver, leaves the children in the shadow of the blackboard and the flannelgraph.

It shines on Frankie, because today he is alone.

A MURDER STORY

By Kenneth Reed

"COME." She led him up the dark path to the cottage. Inside, the warm fogged over his glasses. What a smell! Nory's Grandmom had been baking cookies all day and the table was covered end to end with a marching army of stars, oversized snowmen, fat camels, raisin drop rabbits, and sand tarts.

But the boy also smelled burning wood and the odor of a wet springhouse in summer and horses and there were surely no water tubs or horses here. It seemed out of place in this new house. Apparently the grandparents had moved the smells along in with the furniture from the old farmhouse.

"Grandpop!" He was sitting backwards on a chair, fastening clamps on it to pull its broken back together. He stood up, beaming, and threw his arms around her.

"My, my," and a hand that seemed like it was all knuckles went on patting her on the back.

"Grandpop, that tickles."

"What tickles?" He winked one wrinkled eye at the boy.

"Your beard," and she pulled his wispy beard.

"Hey, what disrespect is this?" and he kissed her. "She hadn't seen me for a week. Shh, your grandmom's asleep."

"Grandpop used to be a preacher," said Nory.

"Used to be? How do you stop?" asked the boy. They never did in his area. They just went on preaching until they had heart attacks in the pulpit or their vocal chords finally petered out.

"I just stopped," said Grandpop, "and told everyone in the church that I'd appreciated them for forty-two years and this was my last Sunday. Then I said the benediction and I never went up in the pulpit again."

"I'm glad you're not a preacher anymore," said Isaac. The old man picked up a tube of glue. "I don't like preachers."

"Isaac!" said Nory.

"It's true, I don't. It's them and dormitory managers that try to push religion into you like an aspirin. Religion is just an aspirin anyway."

"An aspirin?" said the old man.

"Sure. Take one three times a day. A prayer in the morning, a prayer at dinnertime, and a prayer in the evening. It'll cure your problems, make you stop thinking about girls, and take you home to Jesus someday."

Nory's eyes avoided his, but Isaac felt a strange confidence in this old man. Perhaps because the man hadn't said anything yet.

"And you ought to see the boys who pray so beautifully when they get back in the dormitory. They're devils, that's what they are."

"Devils?" said Grandpop, and he looked up from the gluing.

"Yes, devils. They make fun of a fellow's family because he's poor; they throw him in the shower because he reads Karl Marx; they spy on a fellow and report everything to the hall manager. Is that Christian, I want to know? Is that what it's like to be Mennonite?"

"Did you say Mennonite?"

"Sure, they're Mennonites, all of them are. Except maybe Fahnestock. I think he's Episcopalian."

"You mean they were raised in Mennonite homes. They have Mennonite names and their families speak Dutch, maybe. . . ."

"Nobody's family speaks Dutch," said Nory.

"Not anymore? Well, their grandfathers did. That reminds me of a story, but let me finish. Some people think *Mennonite* is a belief, a religion. But it's not. It's a tribe, or maybe a culture," said Grandpop, and he looked up sideways at the boy. He held the glue in one hand and a drop fell out unnoticed and landed on his knee. "There are good Mennonites and bad ones, just as there are good elephants and bad ones. Or good horses and bad ones. I don't think you want to lump them all together." He went back to his gluing.

"But you're right," said Grandpop after awhile. "It's not Christian. There are not good Christians and bad ones. Only bad ones. That's why Paul calls himself the chiefest of sinners. All sinners, all bad Christians, but all trying to do better so God can relax a bit. But Mennonites? Of course there are good Mennonites. Eat the right food, sing the hymns in the right language — "

"Not anymore — " began Nory, but Grandpop went on.

"— don't join the army, wear plain clothes, and run a good farm. Do you know the quickest way to become a bad Mennonite? Don't weed your garden in the summer."

"I like your ideas," said the boy, and he looked at Grandpop with admiration.

"Where did you meet this young fellow?"

"Me?" said Nory. "We're in school together. He was working for Papa this morning."

"I didn't even shake his hand. What's the name."

"Isaac Guthrie."

"Isaac Guthrie. Well, I'll tell you something, Isaac. Her papa's a hard-working man."

"He's about the only high school teacher I like," said the boy.

"Is that true? Oh, I'm glad," said Nory. "No. Don't misunderstand. You should like others too. What about Brother Zook?" She was sitting beside him on the bench at the table, watching Grandpop work.

"Oh, I broke one," said the boy, and he held up two halves of a cookie, shaped like a horse and sprinkled with some sparkling green stuff.

"Eat it, eat it," said Grandpop. "The Mennonites also make good cookies." And he laughed. He was enjoying himself, philosophizing, and it was never more fun than when he had one or two of the "young people" at his knee. They weren't like their parents, who had no time to listen and sat with their hands over their mouths to hide their boredom. No, everything was new to them and their eyes were wide open and curious. "Can I have one, Schnickelfritz?" And Schnickelfritz smiled and gave her grandfather a camel.

"What about the story, Grandpop?" said Nory.

Grandpop got up and put the chair away to dry. He got another chair from the table, sat down and crossed his legs.

"Go check on your grandmother," he said.

"She's still sleeping," said Nory.

"Okay," and Grandpop pulled a fat cigar from his pocket and bit off one end. "She doesn't like me to smoke when there are visitors." He lit it. "But it helps the story."

"And you are a preacher?" said the boy startled. None of the preachers in his area smoked, he was sure of that.

"I was. Also a bad Christian, saved only by the grace of God." The air above the cookie table began to turn blue.

"Well, it's murder. That won't scare you off, will it, Nory? But we don't know about the young fellow here. Frederick Kolb would have been your great-great-grandfather, Nory, because he was my grandfather, and at the time of the murder he was a little older than you, young fellow."

Nory smiled at Isaac suddenly, and he felt like he was being admitted to a close family secret.

"Frederick Kolb was what you and I would call a progressive. Or maybe a rebel, and our people have never loved rebels, even though they began their history as rebels in the Reformation. Frederick was growing up in the time when the Mennonites first began to lose their German. And the Pennsylvania Dutch, what we call the dialect. Oh, they went on preaching it in church and folks my age used it all the time with each other, but the young people were growing up without being able to speak it. They could understand it, you see, but they couldn't speak it. And it was the schools that did it. The little ones heard nothing but the dialect until they got to first grade, just like I did, and after that they heard nothing but English. It just wasn't fun to speak Dutch — I know it was rough — those English boys had a poem when I was in school:

Dutchman, Dutchman, belly full of straw,
Can say nothing but ja ja ja.

So like I say, it wasn't any fun to talk Dutch, because it just made you feel like an oddball. Do you like that poem, do you?" He said it again and laughed. "I couldn't laugh about it then though." The old man puffed and began again with the cigar in one corner of his mouth.

"Frederick was the leader type; he had all kinds of talent. Just like your friend here," he said, looking at the boy. "He started a music school on Sunday nights and the young people went there to sing hymns in English. And they loved it. He met a young girl named Mary Martha from the area and after a while, boom, they got engaged. You see, Frederick was no dummy. He saw the young people weren't getting their hearts warmed one bit at the church services because they couldn't participate. They couldn't sing or testify because they didn't know anything but children's words in Dutch. So they just had to sit tight in church, because everyone there spoke Dutch. 'God Himself speaks the dialect,' one of our deacons used to say.

"But a lot of older folks felt bad about the singings, especially the ones with young children, in their thirties and forties, maybe. They had to sit tight when they were young, you see, but now that they had made it, they wanted to lord it over the younger generation. 'It isn't Christian to sing in English,' they said. 'If you were raised in an English home, yes then you should sing in English, but if you were raised in a Dutch home, you should sing in Dutch.' Now isn't that some reasoning. But the biggest thing was that the young people weren't coming to anything but Sunday morning church anymore and some even stopped coming altogether.

"Some of those older folks were Mary Martha's brother Abe and his wife. They looked around for someone to blame their troubles on and picked Frederick. And Abe told Frederick one day that he had better not appear at the farm again until he joined up with the German-speaking church.

"One night, it was in the summer, I think, Abe and his wife and Mary Martha (she lived with them) decided to step outside the house for a bit. I don't know what for. Maybe they went for a walk after the evening milking. Anyway Abe's wife left their little baby in the crib because she was sleeping and they thought they'd be right back, so they covered her with a little feather quilt and tied a string across it. They'd do that so the baby couldn't get up and fall out of the crib.

"Well, when they came back — they weren't gone over fifteen minutes — they heard a window slam and when they ran upstairs, what do you think they found? The baby was gone. They looked and looked around the house and then they went back to the bedroom and looked again and this time they noticed the mattress was pushed up. They pulled it up and there was that little baby, dead."

"Smothered?" said Isaac.

"Smothered dead."

"A thief?" said the boy.

"Well, Abe's wife was sure Frederick Kolb had killed the baby. 'Because he hated us,' that's what she told folks.

And the next day they found his hat with his name on it on the front porch, just as if he had forgotten it there when he jumped from the window.

"They tried Frederick in court — yes, the Mennonites don't sue in court, they say, but that young father was angry. They couldn't convict him — that is Frederick — they couldn't convict him, and he maintained that he'd been home with the flu the night it happened, but there was no way to prove that either. So Frederick said to dig the child up and 'I'll touch it in the presence of everyone.' But her parents refused, because a month had already passed."

"Why did he want to touch the baby?"

"Superstition. Superstition, girl. But they believed it then. If the murderer touched his victim, some sign of blood would appear; so it also stands to reason if he was innocent, nothing would happen. That was the end of Frederick Kolb. The Mennonite community just dropped him like that. Bang. Like the boys drop a girl when they find out she's not — you know what I mean, young man?"

"But the court?" said the boy.

"They couldn't prove anything one way or the other. That didn't matter to the Mennonites. They all believed he was guilty, even his fiancee. They excommunicated him, and Mary Martha married some other boy who was a good church member." The old man puffed. Isaac reached for another cookie so he could look at Nory. Her eyes were closed and she was leaning against the wall but he could tell she wasn't asleep.

"The story has a happy ending though. The community didn't forgive him, understand. He raised a family and all of his family joined the church, and he attended services himself, but he wasn't a member. They probably would have buried him in the Lutheran plot in town.

"But when he was seventy years old, a strange thing happened. Someone telephoned him and told him to come to the hospital out in Juniata County real quick. They'd found the man who did the murder, and he'd confessed, praise the Lord. Frederick caught a train, but he got there too late. The man was dead, but folks reported his last words were, "Tell Frederick I'm sorry.' It turned out to be Mary Martha's other boyfriend years ago, and he was so jealous when Frederick won the race, so to speak, that he decided to ruin his reputation.

"All those years that man was a church member, but they say he lived the last ten years of his life in agony because of 'horrible things I've done.' That's how he said it. 'Horrible things I've done.' "

"That's not a very happy ending."

"Sure it is. Frederick was *innocent*, and now they could all see it. I can remember my grandfather saying again and again when I was younger, 'I'd give my right hand to tell him I forgive him.' "

"Forgive him!" said the boy with unbelief.

"Yes."

"Why should he forgive him?"

"Because Frederick was a Christian. Forgiveness, Isaac, that's the here and the there of the Christian." He hit one side of the table and then the other. "And everything in between. I don't care about your good Mennonites one bit," and he hit the table right in the middle with his fist. A cookie fell off and broke into twelve pieces.

There was a stirring in the next room. Grandpop took the cigar stub out of his mouth and put it out on the sole of his shoe. It was scarred.

The door opened and there were the piercing eyes of Grandmother. She walked into the room and her breasts galloped on the expansive stomach that proclaimed years of eating her own pies and bearing babies for Grandpop. Her hair fell straight and gray below her waist with a few combs in place on top to hold the center part while it dried. Her traditional-size prayer veil was not pinned on but only perching — she had slipped it on when she heard strange voices.

"Pa! Not in front of your visitors again," she said loudly. "What kind of a preacher are you?"

Grandpop pushed the broken cookie under the table with one foot and looked at the boy. His eyes were full of delight.

"But I wouldn't have anything but a Mennnonite wife," he said.

THE HEAVY LOAD

By Merle Good

JOHN MILLER dropped his flashlight on the grass and jumped over the edge of the bank into the water. He reached for the light and snapped it on as he turned toward the muskrat slide. The trap was snapped.

"Well, I'll be Jehosphat's neighbor-in-law!" he muttered. He held in his hand a sawed-off broom handle with a hook in the end. He used it to pull traps out of the water. "How in the world did that trap get snapped again?"

John wasn't doing so well this year. Last season he'd caught fifty-seven muskrats. That ranked tops on his record. He generally averaged about forty a year. But this year he'd caught only three rats, all in the same morning. Other mornings he found several of his traps snapped but no sign of the fur-bearing animals.

John's dad had suggested checking the traps before dawn. So this morning he had gotten up at two o'clock. But things were no different. Four of the first ten traps were sprung.

John pulled the trap out of the water and reset it. One more try, he decided. He slipped off his leather glove and leaned down, his fingers stinging in the cold water as he pushed the trap in place at the bottom of the slide.

He wiped his hand against his coat, then jammed his icy fingers into the stiff leather. He reached to grab the bank shoulder to pull himself up out of the water. Suddenly he stopped. In the moonlight he saw footmarks in the frost. Funny thing, he thought. He hadn't noticed them before. Of course, looking out across the meadow from this angle made the frost appear quite white. And the tracks, in contrast, were a deep green.

John had suspected a thief for several days. Now he was sure of it. He saw the tracks lead down along the bank toward the woods where most of his traps were set.

John thought quickly. He always checked this side on the way down and the other side on the way home. He reached for his flashlight and waded across the stream to the other side. The light showed the frost on the opposite bank sparkling white and undisturbed by tracks.

John pulled himself up on the bank and ran to his nearest trap. He whistled softly as the beam of light showed a broad flat tail floating behind the trap. "Well, I'll be Jehoshaphat's grandma!" he chuckled. The muskrat had drowned.

In a moment he had the trap on the bank. He reached to push its jaws apart. But then he stopped. He snapped off the flashlight and turned toward the woods, eyes searching for a trace of light. After several minutes he saw it

— a faint flash in the water.

John pushed the jaws apart, threw the unset trap into the water, and laid the muskrat on the bank beside the stake marking the trap. He turned and ran into a clump of trees several yards away.

John thought while he waited. Christians are men of divided purpose. John was no exception.

The light came closer as he deliberated. It would stop, flash into the water, and then go on. Twice the thief paused long enough to pull another muskrat from a trap.

Then he was at the last trap. He paused, flashed, and came on toward the muskrat on the bank. John looked hard. He didn't recognize him. Probably someone from town, he decided.

The thief halted abruptly over the muskrat. Then swiftly he shone his light into the water, across to the other bank, and back across the meadow.

Finally he turned his flashlight on the clump of trees. John knew he saw him, but that didn't matter. His decision was made. He stepped out from the trees and walked toward the thief.

He stopped a yardstick's length from the bearded man. He sensed fear, suspicion in his eyes.

John smiled when he saw the bulging bag the thief held. A dozen rats at least, he guessed. A dozen rats times eight equaled a few too many to think about. John spoke.

"You're a strong man to carry such a heavy load. Here, let me put this one in."

A VISION OF APOCALPYSE

By J. D. Stahl

THE MEETING of the Jesus people was held outdoors in an open, grassy space close to the highway. A few picnic benches sat scattered under the trees along the edge of the small park. Shortly after dark, when Pastor Hartman arrived, the meeting was in full swing. A rock band played and the forty or so Jesus people had formed a circle as they sang, "I love my Jesus, yeah!" They moved freely to the music, dancing in a circle with hands clasped, and then clapping and shouting.

Down the road a hundred yards high-powered cars roared in and out of the parking lot of the Tropical Treat. Beneath the deep sea-blue sky orange taillights glowed and tires squealed. Laughter and whistles mixed in the tar-scented air.

The group beneath the trees paid no attention to the traffic and occasional catcalls from the Tropical Treat. The dancers widened the circle to receive newcomers. Pastor Hartman stood a bit aside in the shadow of a canopy to watch. A number of curious onlookers shared the shadows with him.

The group sang with gusto. Their exuberance impressed Pastor Hartman. Even more, he liked the variety of people there. It did his heart good to see an old man with a stoop and a wrinkled smile beside a young black man, a fuzzy-haired head bobbing next to a girl with a prayer covering, whom he recognized as a girl from his congregation.

The circle broke and the group stood around in clusters as a young man with long blond hair told how he had been freed from the power of drugs.

A girl with a kind, open face came up to Pastor Hartman.

"I'm Ruth. What is your name?" she asked, beaming at him, standing halfway in the light of an unshielded bulb.

"Enos Hartman. Call me Enos."

"Are you a Christian?"

"Yes, I'm glad to say I am," Enos smiled back. Ruth beamed even more and would have embraced him if he hadn't held back a little.

The young man with a headband and a flowing, colorful shirt spoke fervently: "I know the power of God! I've seen it! I've felt it! He's got the power to make us whole. He can make us free — free from slavery. Some of us have been slaves — some of you are slaves. I don't mean slaves to some man. I mean slaves to drugs, to lust, to yourself. But you can be free! That's what it's all about! Praise the Lord!" The audience cheered.

Someone struck up a song and the rest joined in with

spirit. Enos had never heard the song before, but he liked it very much. It spoke of joy and freedom, and he thought that as far as he could see the young people around him had joy and freedom.

A commotion began at the other end of the picnic grounds during the song. A knot of people formed and Enos faintly heard chants.

"It will be all right." Ruth shook her head. "They are driving the demon out of Joyce. She's been possessed. You can come watch, and pray, if you like." She took his hand and led him in the direction of the huddle.

A figure lay on the grass in the shadows, pinned down by two persons bending over her holding her arms. Eight or ten of the Jesus people surrounded the motionless body, chanting and holding Bibles and small crosses over her at arm's length.

Suddenly the figure began to writhe and moan. The huddle moved closer together so that she could hardly be seen anymore. They began to sing.

"They won't hurt her, will they?" Enos asked with consternation.

"It always hurts to drive the devil out," Ruth said glancing at him with a serious expression.

"But they know what they are doing, don't they?"

Ruth did not answer. Enos had mixed feelings about the scene before him. He distrusted the shadows and the way the girl was being held down and surrounded.

Ruth joined the others around the possessed girl. The rock band still blared away. Noise from cars passing on the highway mixed with the singing and shouting. The girl on the ground began to scream in fits.

Enos hesitated, undecided on what he ought to do. He looked around him to see what the rest of the group was doing. Some were wandering about; others had formed small knots to discuss or persuade. The band played on. A tall and lanky girl sang into the microphone. Her voice sounded tinny over the loudspeakers.

Pastor Hartman felt helpless. He could not formulate clear alternatives in his mind. Perhaps he had better leave, he thought, but that did not seem right either. He turned back to Ruth. Maybe he ought to talk to her some more. He moved in her direction. Shouts and singing rose from the closed circle.

Suddenly, a tremendous crashing noise from behind startled Enos. Two cars had just collided on the highway. Enos turned in terror to see the hulks of the two vehicles whirl around in a furious spinning motion. Both cars had been passing in the center lane of the three-lane highway when they caught each other almost head-on at high speed. The careening cars were sent down over opposite banks by the impetus of their crash.

Enos stood paralyzed. Chills ran over his body. Some of the Jesus people ran wildly toward the highway where the cars had left the road. Others ran down the road to the Tropical Treat to phone for help.

The first thing Enos thought of was the story of Jesus and the man possessed by demons, called Legion. When Christ drove the evil spirits out of Legion, they fled into a herd of pigs and caused them to run into the sea and drown.

But the circle before Enos still bent over the demon-possessed girl, whom Ruth had called Joyce, chanting and praying, as the traffic began to line up for miles on each side waiting for the road to be cleared. Fire trucks and ambulances roared and wailed to the scene of the accident. Spotlights were pointed at the wrecks and rescue squads piled out of the trucks to give emergency aid.

Competing with sirens and truck motors, the songs and prayers still sounded into the cool night air, though now the night was made bright by an endless line of head-lights and the flashing red and blue signal lamps.

Shattered glass lay sprayed across the highway. Onlookers crowded the banks. Torches burned and sawed away at car roofs. Screams of the wounded and perhaps dying mixed with screams of the tortured soul struggling on the ground as voices chanted above her.

It struck Enos like a scene of apocalypse. He felt dwarfed by terrible events without explanation. Most of all he felt helpless, powerless, afraid.

People from nearby homes began to cross the overpass between the flood-lamp-lit picnic ground and the now nearly deserted Tropical Treat, curious and intent on the spectacle, some of them in night robes.

A feeling of unreality passed over Enos. He felt faint for a moment. Perhaps it was only a bad dream.

As suddenly as the feeling came it was gone again. All at once his head was clear. He looked around him. The grass bank around the wreck was tinted greenish-blue by torches. Enos felt a sudden wave of disgust at the crowd of onlookers. They seemed useless, a hindrance, only trying to satisfy their lust for spectacle.

Then he realized that he was a spectator too. He turned back to the group over the girl, Joyce. Now he knew what his choice was. Either he must leave at once, or he must take decisive action.

His misgivings about the situation before him were clearer now too. *Juvenile nonsense, this waving of Bibles and symbols,* he thought. *Dramatic self-indulgence.*

He stepped into the circle.

"Silence," he commanded. His voice expressed conviction. "Let me talk to her."

The group was silent. Enos knelt beside Joyce and took her arms out of the grip holding them.

"My name is Enos," he said quietly to her. "I want to talk to you alone. Are you all right?"

Joyce's eyes were closed, her hair stringy with sweat. Enos looked up. Blank faces stared back at him. Joyce's body was limp; if he let her go she would flop down to the ground again. Then he caught Ruth's eye.

"Help me take her over to the bench," Enos pleaded. For a moment he felt the old helplessness resurging. *What if he had interrupted a real casting out of demons? What if Joyce would not respond at all?*

Ruth pushed some people aside who stood in her way. Together Ruth and Enos lifted Joyce and led her over to a deserted bench. Most of the group stood motionless and watched. A few followed; but when Enos looked at them questioningly they retreated.

"I'm here to help you," Enos began. His voice was soothing. He smiled at himself; he knew he was being parental. "You need a warm meal and a good rest."

Ruth looked a little puzzled. Joyce did not respond. Ruth took Joyce's face between her hands and said insistently, "Joyce, do you hear?"

Even Enos was surprised when Joyce opened her eyes. He was so glad he just sat there oblivious to everything else for a while. Then he said, "My wife is waiting for me. She'll be glad to heat some food for you. We have a place where you can stay — or do you have a home?"

Joyce shook her head. She looked tired and dazed.

"Would you like to come?" Enos asked.

Joyce nodded.

Enos had long forgotten the various noises surrounding him.

Before he rose to take Joyce to the car with him, he sat for a few moments, silent and thankful that he no longer felt the freezing helplessness he had earlier experienced in the face of his own fear.

GERTIE

by Lois Leatherman

GERTIE LAUSCH stared through the yellowed garret pane. She pointed her uneven nose toward the taped cracks in the glass and directed her eyes beneath the lines of grayish Monday morning sheets to the alley. Her quick glance revealed nothing on the junk heaps worth going down the three flights of creaking stairs to salvage. Gertie sank back into the rocker which she had pulled with a tired zircon-ringed hand from its position on the other side of a musty-smelling mattress.

Gertie was tired. Tired of being sixty-eight and tired of being furtive when she slipped through the streets in search of pretty trinkets to put in her cardboard box. Tired of being alone. Gertie was tired of remembering the days when her lipstick went loudly red on sensuous lips instead of turning purple on thin lines of dryness that even Cheryl Henselee's Miracle Cream didn't penetrate.

Gertie sighed for the movement of ragtime in her bony legs and the flirtatious "H'ya, girlie!" floating in one ear and out the other as she hurried with restless abandon from her job at Bob's Luncheonette to a night life with Hank or Ralph or Ben of the padlock company.

But Gertie didn't let herself remember very much. The lumpy mattress and winding stairs and welfare checks were more pleasant if she thought of something new like the little piece of red silk she'd found in Smiths' backyard or the plastic ring with the painting of curly-haired Shirley Temple. Today she would go searching for other pretty objects but not until Mrs. Landis came bouncing up the steps with a bright smile and a dozen eggs and some fruit or canned soup tied up in a bow of bright green ribbon and lined with pages from old religious magazines.

Mrs. Landis's first name was Charity. Gertie really liked Charity. Sometimes Charity would come all alone to listen to Gertie talk and other times she brought her twelve-year-old daughter along. The two would sit and smile as Gertie told them about the contents of her cardboard box or about how the three geraniums in her backyard were doing.

Gertie was always careful not to reminisce about her gay youth when Charity's daughter was with her, and Charity rewarded her once by taking her out to dinner. Gertie smiled a toothless smile when she thought of the embarrassed way Mrs. Landis turned her head when she started telling what she had been doing at forty. Gertie was glad two people who had lived such different lives could be friends. Charity had even thanked her sweetly for offering to let her have the elegant old brooch in the cardboard box to accent the simple black dress she'd worn to the restaurant.

Today Charity was going to come at about ten o'clock before she went off to a meeting of the Missionary Sewing Club. That would give Gertie time to take a lazy walk to the drugstore for some arthritis pills before she sat down to sip her potato soup. Gertie rocked slowly and listened to the creaking arms of the chair. She tapped a red fingernail on the windowsill until she heard the familiar sound of Mrs. Landis's stiletto heels on the front porch. The slow scrape of Mrs. Landis's market basket against the walls made the plaster fall in little heaps. Mrs. Landis knocked three brisk gloved knocks before she opened the door and called out a cherry "Gertie?"

Gertie nodded "hello" as Mrs. Landis set the basket on the narrow dresser top.

"I thought I'd come a little earlier today because I want to see Sally Greeves before the meeting. How are you feeling this week?"

"Okay."

"Do the joints in your fingers still pain you so? My doctor says there is a better medicine out now. I could probably get you some in town on Friday."

"S'better. I got me some new beads and I'm still savin' up my money for that coat with a furry collar. That'll be warm and purty. Don't you think so?"

"I'm sure. But we have to be careful how we spend our money these days. You are careful, aren't you, Gertie?"

"I get me whut I needs and I get me whut I wants to be happy with."

"I see."

"Wanta see my new beads? Paid ten dollars for them. Look like real pearls." She minced toward the cardboard box set on a high shelf of the dingy closet. Tenderly and with slow stretching movements she reached for the box and smiled quickly as she opened it. Her fingers moved with deliberate salesgirl elegance toward the necklace and held a midair pose for a few seconds till Mrs. Landis stepped closer to admire the whiteness and delicate roundness of the beads.

Gertie thought Mrs. Landis should have smiled more. Instead she looked worried and cleared her throat before she said, "I suppose it's all right as long as you keep on paying the rent and have enough to eat. We all have our ways of bringing a ray of light to our dark corners. Maybe you better put them away. I really must go see Sally. And if your fingers keep hurting you, be sure to tell me next week and I'll pick up that medicine."

Gertie wished Mrs. Landis hadn't gone down the steps in such a flurry. It would have been nice to talk to someone for a while before walking alone to the drugstore. Gertie reached into the closet once more to exchange her torn housecoat for a red and white gingham blouse and a brown skirt that was too loose and too long. She liked to wear it often because she once saw Jane Wyman wearing one just like it in an old movie at the Grand. She groped in the pockets of her gray coat to see if the five-dollar bill was still there. It was, so she closed the closet door the whole way so nobody would see the cardboard box. Then she took a long slow look in the dirty mirror and powdered her nose with a threadbare puff.

It would take her fifteen minutes to walk to the drugstore and she would stop at the pawnshop afterward to look at the pretty things. Gertie wasn't sure what she'd do after lunch. Maybe take a walk in the park and try to find that old man with the bent cigar.

She'd seen him sitting there alone many times and once she sat on the same bench with him and didn't say anything. He just kept puffing on his cigar and looked straight ahead and was very grim. Gertie felt a young and spry sixty-eight in comparison to him. She would have guessed him to be eighty or even more. Gertie put her foot on the first step and grasped the handrail to guide her down the stairs.

At the drugstore she paid for her pills and put a dime in the March of Dimes box and bought a piece of bubble gum for a penny because it came with a ring. She was chewing her gum when she walked into the pawnshop and saw the old man looking at some dust-covered books. Gertie stopped beside him and pretended to read.

"Hullo. You come in here often?"

"No."

"Just wondered. I never seen you here before. I come here every day." Gertie waited while the old man limped toward the door. Then she called out after him. "You goin' to the park?"

He nodded.

"Think I'll come along." Gertie and the old man walked to the place in the park where the pigeons were eating and found an empty bench.

The old man never said very much but Gertie asked him what his name was and he replied a groggy "Max."

Gertie just looked at her pigeons and chewed her gum. She showed Max the ring she got and he expressed a mild interest in the picture of Niagara Falls (that's what he said it was) printed on the plastic. When Gertie left to go home for lunch she felt very quiet and after she had eaten her soup she lay back on her bed and took a long peaceful nap. When she woke she went to her closet and took out

Gertie and the old man walked to the place in the park
where the pigeons were eating and found an empty bench.

the cardboard box and put the ring with the picture of Niagara Falls on top of the one with the picture of Shirley Temple. Then she went out to look on the gravel of the alley to see if she could find anything new for her box. She couldn't, but that didn't make her feel bad. When it was six o'clock she put her ear up to the wall separating her from the next apartment and listened to piano music cracking from an old radio. She always did that.

Gertie Lausch always got up early in the mornings too. And she always went to the pawnshop with a little money and she always took walks in the park. The next week, between times when Mrs. Landis would come to talk, Gertie went every day to talk to Max on the park bench. Each morning before she left the room, she would take something from the box with her and Max would not say anything at all when she sat beside him. Except after a while . . . he would look at what she had brought and say whether or not the picture on it was of something he knew or whether the trinket was made of plastic or metal or of silk or cotton. Gertie was glad he knew such things.

Sunday while Gertie was sitting beside Max on the park bench, she thought all at once that maybe he would like to come see her cardboard box and tell her about everything in it. They could have tomato soup for supper. Max came. He sat impassively in Gertie's rocker and said a few words about each of her trinkets. Gertie sat on the lumpy mattress and stared at the window beyond Max's feeble white head. At six o'clock both Gertie and Max listened to the radio through the wall. Max didn't stay awake very long. Gertie put a cushion behind his head so he wouldn't wake up by rolling it against the hard back of the rocker.

Then she tiptoed out the door and went to the drug-store to buy some cigars for five cents apiece. Max didn't move much at all, but the next morning when he woke he watched the neighborhood women hang out their wash on pulleys between the tenement houses. Gertie thought he looked surprised to see Mrs. Landis pop in the door at eight in the morning. She had forgotten to tell him Charity was going to be coming with soup and eggs.

Gertie thought Charity looked even more surprised to see Max. "He's my cousin," Gertie lied. "He's going to stay here a while." Charity peered at Max's dirty brown shirt and gray dungarees. Gertie thought she looked worried again.

"You really don't have room for him here, do you? I mean there's no space for a cot."

Gertie nodded agreement. There was no space for a cot. "We'll have to do without, I guess."

Gertie watched Charity turn nervously around in the small room. She seemed to be in a hurry, so Gertie told her to go ahead. It was okay if she didn't have time to talk this morning since Max was here.

"Gertie, surely you know he can't stay. I know the landlord won't want an extra boarder. And, he's not your cousin, is he?"

Gertie said he wasn't. Mrs. Landis turned around so swiftly as she left the room, that her heel tore a deeper hole in the cracked maroon linoleum. Gertie noticed that she forgot to leave the basket with the eggs and soup. Gertie almost called after her at the top of the stairwell, but something about the way Mrs. Landis was twisting her white glove made Gertie close her mouth.

Gertie paused to look at Max before she reached up into the closet to get out her cardboard box. She grabbed clumsily at the beads and put them into her coat pocket as she slung its loose heaviness over her shoulder. "Max," Gertie said, "I'll be back. I gotta go to the store to get us some groceries for this week." Gertie fingered the beads in her pocket before she put her hand on the banister.

THE PRESENT STRENGTH

By J. D. Stahl

JAMES spread the map of Berlin out on the table before him and studied it. He had an address on a small card with the list of street names and found the coordinates. Then he searched the map and put his finger on the spot when he located the street he was looking for. He glanced at his watch. It was time for him to leave. He swung into his coat and patted his pocket to make sure the car keys were there. On the sidewalk he stopped for a moment to look up at the starry cloudless night sky.

Lights from the shop windows flashed through the car as he accelerated and slowed from block to block, nearing the center of the city. The familiar scent and sound of the VW bug reassured him. Traffic was not heavy. As he braked the car to a stop, seeing a red light ahead of him, he glanced over at the curb. In the shadows of an entranceway two prostitutes posed. One of them lifted her hand to the orange swirl of curls at her forehead with a negligent gesture and impulsively pushed herself out of the shadow into the neon night, towards the VW. At each step she twisted the narrow band of cloth circling her hips with an exaggerated motion. She reached for the car door but James' hand flicked out and hit the lock button a moment before. She wrenched the handle angrily, then beat her fingers against the window in a furious staccato. Her hideous long fingernails were painted black like dried blood.

James peered up at the traffic light. It shone a forbidding red. The girl bent down and looked into the car. She bared her teeth in a silent ugly grin and winked at him. James reached over and rolled the window down a fraction. "I'm sorry, I'm not taking anyone along," James told her in a voice that allowed no argument. She forced her fingers through the slit in reply but hurt herself and tried to yank her hand back out, breaking one of the long black fingernails. She cursed. James shook his head and reached into his inside coat pocket and pulled out a piece of paper and offered it to her through the window opening. "This is all I can give you," he said, and at the same moment, mercifully, the light changed. She snatched it with a scowl and he let the car jump forward.

God's Plan for Your Life, the tract said in bold letters. James glanced at the street corner in his rearview mirror and saw the girl jump back to the curb to avoid being hit by a car, crumple the paper in her fist and shake it at him and stamp her foot.

A sharp winding curve led James into a silent street lined by mansions and well-kept yards. The wealth of the neighborhood was evident as James stepped onto the sidewalk and approached the house, checking his destination on the little card from his wallet with the number on the stone wall circling the garden. A metal plate with a grill was lit by a bell button and name sign. The gate was locked. James pressed the button and a moment later a buzz released the gate and he walked up the path to the house. A woman was standing in the doorway framed in light.

"Mr. Schlabach?" she asked.

"Yes. And you are Mrs. Helmuth?" he asked and shook her offered hand.

"No, I'm her sister. My husband and I are here to calm her. I'll show you in."

When James stepped into the living room he stopped in surprise. Its garishness overwhelmed him. The colors were reds and greens and the furniture was modernistic — sinuous, bold, plastic shapes bathed in bright harsh light. On the far side of the large room a gray-haired man and a woman with formal bearing sat in separate cubicle-like armchairs of white plastic. A disturbingly patterned rug covered the floor and one entire wall. On the opposite wall a glass and metal cupboard held an array of electronic machinery and a cold gray TV eye.

The man and woman rose and the woman came toward him haltingly. "Thank you for coming, Mr. Schlabach. Not only for my sake; my husband would have been pleased, too, I am sure." She stopped. Her face was sagging and every motion betrayed her anxiety.

The man introduced himself and begged James to sit down. "My name is Mr. Weinreich," he said. "I am the brother-in-law. Would you like something to drink or smoke?" James refused politely. Mrs. Helmuth lit a cigarette.

"I came to talk to you about what I am going to say tomorrow," James began. I haven't ever done anything like this before, so I probably know as little as you what to expect. Perhaps you can tell me a bit about Mr. Helmuth first."

The three people surveyed James carefully, his youthful face framed by a trim black beard, his coat cut like a clerical collar, his strong hands and his rather formal pose. Mr. Weinreich cleared his throat and said: "Mr. Helmuth was a professor at the university. We assumed you knew that. By the way, young man, what is your profession? I don't believe we were told. You belong to the freethinkers. That is all we know."

James looked at him in amazement. "Freethinkers! No, you are mistaken. I belong to one of the free churches, as they are called here. I am a missionary and preacher of the Beachy Amish Church, from America."

Everyone stood up without being conscious of it. Mr. Weinreich lost his composure. "Oh, this is really a stupid affair. There must have been a misunderstanding somewhere. We were told on the phone that we would be sent a speaker from a freethinking society, something like a philosopher, someone who knows how to give appropriate thoughts for occasions such as ours. We simply did not want some priest to give his routine drivel over the coffin of our — this is very annoying. I'm sure it is not your fault, Mr. — , Mr. Schlabach but — " He stopped, uncertain what to do.

Mrs. Helmuth broke in: "We hardly have time to get another speaker by tomorrow afternoon anymore, do we?"

"I'm sorry about this too," James joined in.

"Why don't you stay a little and tell us what you had planned?" Mrs. Helmuth asked. "What kind of a church is it that you come from? I forgot what you called it. Maybe he could speak tomorrow anyway, Werner." She turned to Mr. Weinreich and lowered her voice. "He doesn't look like an ordinary state-church pastor, does he?"

James sat down again. "I hadn't planned what I was going to say tomorrow. I want to let the Spirit lead me. I often can't tell before I begin what I am going to say. But my message is that God is a real and living God and that He has a meaning for our lives. I don't plan to eulogize your husband if you decide to have me speak. Perhaps, if you want me to, I will summarize his life from what you tell me about him, but then I will simply share what God wants me to say."

Mrs. Helmuth tapped her cigarette ash into the ashtray and then took it to her lips, inhaling deeply. The smoke made her pinch her eyes together. She exchanged glances with Mr. Weinreich.

"My church is Anabaptist, if that means anything to you."

Mrs. Helmuth nodded.

"But the important thing I have to say is that our human lives can have meaning through a relationship with God. I am not an educated person. I can't argue with you philosophically. But what I have to say is easy to understand because it is real. It's something I couldn't talk about if I did not experience it every day."

"What do you do, Mr. Schlabach, in your work here in Berlin?" Mr. Weinreich did not sound too unfriendly. His wife went over to the cupboard, slid a panel aside, laid out a tray of cakes, and offered coffee.

James took a cup. "Until recently I was pastor of a small congregation here in Berlin. After almost five years it had become quite familiar and warm. But, both my wife and I began to feel that perhaps it was too safe, too familiar. We sensed the leading of the Lord to look for some other work, here in Berlin. We felt called to help drug addicts and alcoholics. Some of them had come to our services at the congregation occasionally, but we never had enough time to really help them get free from their bondage, and they felt like strangers in our close-knit congregation. It was hard to leave, especially for my wife, who felt the need for a place with security and warmth like we had there.

"So we asked God to show us His will and give us a house if He wanted us to move. We waited for a time, a number of months, and then one of our co-workers came to us with a newspaper ad and said, maybe this is God's answer. It looked just right, a house at the outskirts of the city. The price was not too high, so we went to see it. It was really exciting. The place we found was exactly fitted to our needs. There was plenty of space and the possibility of doing some renovation and expansion to make it a home for the people we wanted to help. So we telephoned our mission board in America. They telegraphed back that the budget was completely depleted but that we should go ahead if we felt it was the Lord's will and they would take out a loan to cover the expense of buying the house. Again we had a difficult choice facing us.

"Then someone suggested that we offer to buy the house at a price and let the response from the owner be our answer. We prayed about it again, and decided that it was God's will. So we called the proprietor and made him an offer. He said he would consider it and call us back. We discovered later that he had two offers at the same time, ours and another one from a rich business-man, and that the other offer was higher. But he called us and said he would sell it to us at our price. So we rejoiced and thanked God. Now we are living in the new house and sharing it with fifteen people, young people on parole who had been using drugs and men who are fighting the influence the devil has over them with alcohol. Alcohol can have great power over people's lives. And drugs can too. But with God's help the power of these things can be overcome."

James stopped, disturbed because Mrs. Helmuth had begun to cry and was hiding her face, trying to stifle her sobs.

"Mr. Helmuth died of an overdose of drugs," Mr. Weinreich said in a low voice.

The woman lifted her head, holding one hand to shade her eyes. "Go on, Mr. Schlabach. I want to hear what else you have to say."

James hesitated, then asked Mrs. Weinreich on the other side of the room, "Could you bring me that Bible?" He motioned toward a shelf behind her. "I'd like to use it if I may." She brought it to him. He turned to Matthew 11:28-30 and read, 'Come unto me, all ye that labour and are heavy laden, and I will give you rest. Take my yoke upon you, and learn of me; for I am meek and lowly in heart: and ye shall find rest unto your souls. For my yoke is easy, and my burden is light.' "

"You don't teach the new theology, do you, Mr. Schlabach?" Mr. Weinreich said, smiling a little. "I think we shall have you speak tomorrow despite our little misunderstanding, even if we don't have the same faith as you do. You have something other than philosophy, but maybe that's all right. What do you think, Anna?" The woman nodded without looking up.

An hour and a half later, as James was leaving, Mr.

Weinreich accompanied him out into the hallway. Standing there in the half-shadow by the coat rack he took James' arm and said, "Please be careful what you say tomorrow, for Mrs. Helmuth's sake. What I couldn't tell you out there in the living room was that we are not certain whether her husband took too many pills intentionally or not. He had an addiction that came about gradually from taking pills to alleviate nervousness. The reason I ask you to be considerate in what you say is that Mrs. Helmuth has the same habit, though she will not admit it."

There was a pause and the two men searched each other's faces. It suddenly occurred to both of them how frighteningly soon trust was given and demanded.

"And there's another thing," Mr. Weinreich continued. "You'll probably notice tomorrow. There is a feud in the family, from a long time back, between the relatives of Mr. Helmuth and those of Mrs. Helmuth. It is like a small war. I hope that nothing happens tomorrow, but I feel that I must warn you. Prepare yourself for a shock." Mr. Weinreich's eyes were serious. "I don't know how to express it," he said, "But I sense that you have real strength within you, the kind of strength we need." He reached out and took James' hand in a warm grip.

THE NEXT afternoon, James sat at his desk and studied. He knew he would have to leave soon and he checked the clock on the wall from time to time. He became absorbed in his reading for a while and when he looked up it was suddenly past time to go. He grabbed his coat and clattered down the stairs. As he drove across the city, he wondered what kind of audience would await him. He turned the car into the small parking lot beside the chapel.

The wheels crunched on the gravel. He looked at his watch. He was just on time.

He jumped out of the car and slammed the door shut. And then something struck him. There were no cars in the lot! Only a few near-bare trees fluttered some straggly leaves down to the ground. He stood for a moment without moving. Could he have come to the wrong place? He ran around to the entrance. He pulled the massive door open. It was unlocked. But the chapel was empty. And then he remembered. Lost in thought, he had driven to the wrong chapel.

He raced across the lot to his car and slid into the front seat. Breathless, he slammed the car door, leaned his forehead on the steering wheel, whispering, "Protect me, Lord!" He ground the   starter. The motor leaped into life and the car swung back and around with a roar. James seldom drove so fast. He brought the car to a screechy stop at the right chapel and hurried into the anteroom.

He struggled into the talar, the long black robe worn by clergy on such occasions, and buttoned the vestment with one hand as he flipped through the pages of his Bible with the other. With his heart beating fiercely he crossed to the door leading into the chapel and walked out to the pulpit just as the organist played the final phrase of the introduction and the music ended.

The audience looked at James expectantly as he faced them. He thought, *If you people only knew how I feel inside!* But he began to read with the appearance of calmness. Even as he read he began to feel the tension in the air. It seemed that at any moment, someone might jump up and attack someone else embroiling everyone in a fight. The mourners on the right side of the chapel glowered at those on the left side. The only thing preventing the hostility from becoming physical was the faint reminder that, after all, they were attending a funeral.

The smell of lilies hung in the air with a sickening pungency. James looked out over his bitter audience and prayed for strength and guidance. He had not prepared his text. The tension of the vicious hatred in the room made his pulse race and anxiety grabbed at his knees. What could he say to such an audience? He could not talk about the dead man. To do so would only aggravate the explosive atmosphere.

He found himself reading from the Sermon on the Mount. As he read, he drew strength from the message. He felt the power of the Holy Spirit present, supporting him, and his words took on new confidence. As he read, 'Blessed are the peacemakers,' he looked out across the hostile faces and suddenly there was a response. Some avoided his eyes. Some suddenly seemed to realize that they were at a funeral and that death would be their fate someday too. And as James read on and began to speak, the tension gradually left the room and a new Presence took its place. They were beginning to listen to his words, to watch him carefully. Some of these guests had not come to mourn. Some of them had probably even been glad that the man was gone and out of their way.

James spoke of his own life, and he spoke to the living. He sensed that some were even reaching out trying to understand what he had to say. Afterwards, outside the chapel, a few listeners stopped and talked to him. The widow stood at the driveway and waited her turn. She did not talk loudly and seemed to hesitate every few sentences. She confided that she had a problem with drugs, but she realized this was not the real problem. She admitted something important was missing in her life and had been missing in her husband's life. Now, after his death, things would be even worse.

James listened to her and then told her what he believed God could do in her and how to go about letting Him do it.

Then Mr. Weinreich joined them. As they said farewell, he turned to James and shook his hand. "Thank you for bringing us your strength, Mr. Schlabach," he said.

"It's not my strength," James said, and smiled.

THE FARM AND THE GIRL

By Merle Good

AS RIC TURNED off the highway, his old convertible idled to a lazy halt beside the mailbox standing there in the moonlight. The paint was streaky and the hinge was broken, but he could still read the old man's name. The trio of persimmon trees, guarding long corn rows, threw casual shadows on the grass and weeds that grew at random in the unkept triangle where the road met the lane. Below the lane the small tobacco plants spread leafy palms moonward. Then he smelled the alfalfa in the field down by the creek.

He snapped off the engine and stepped from car to field. He scooped his fingers full of soft, warm earth and pushed closed eyes and lips against the soil.

"By God," he said, "this is my land."

He slipped back into the bucket seat and turned the key. The engine rumbled softly in the evening quiet. But the rumble in his heart was not so quiet. Coming home without Pat was not easy.

But he must go. The old man would be waiting. Ric's mother used to do the waiting. But not tonight. Or ever again for that matter. Cancer was a frightful thing. He knew the little white stone with "Martha" on its flat surface still lay there between the trees, but the weeds this spring had covered it. Shameful weeds. Maybe in a day or so, or at least before the summer ended, he could trim the triangle and tidy up the stone.

The lane ran in along the fields to where the barn doors were propped open, a load of fresh alfalfa backed against the mow. The garage door was open, too, which meant the old man was expecting him. He pulled in beside his father's Olds. He noticed the big car's paint, scratched and faded. Somehow in the year since Martha had died, the old man had lost all the spic-and-span she'd taught him.

Ric glanced beside him at the empty seat and sighed. Pat. If only she were here as she'd been last night. He remembered the wet of hot tears as she lay in his arms, sobbing. It had surprised him that she'd broken down. She must have loved him after all. Pat was a strong girl. Strong, stubborn, and kind. She wanted him to leave the farm. Leave the farm and pursue music and learn to like the city. Her city. She never liked the old man and the old man never liked her. They both wanted him.

The old man said he never should have let Ric go away to school. Then he wouldn't have learned to like piano and the girl wouldn't have tried to take him from the farm.

The old man worked hard. He'd bought the farm during the war. The soil was rundown, grown high in weeds, the buildings shacky, drab, and musty. But the old man and Martha had harnessed the farm and had built a garden out of weeds. Martha planted lilacs and roses, landscaping large lawns above the house, and built the terrace by the creek with its arbors there below the porch. The old man contoured the hills in corn, alfalfa, and tobacco. The cows had held them close to the farm, and the three of them had worked hard. And liked it.

Then cancer came and put the little stone in the triangle near the mailbox. When Martha left, the old man nearly died himself. He milked the cows in silence. He mowed alfalfa slowly, not noticing patchy strips he missed. He hadn't even come to Ric's graduation last spring. He wandered like a stranger about the farm. He seldom spoke, and when he did, his voice was full of weariness.

Then the agriculture scholarship had come. The old man listened quietly and said he'd try to hire someone for the winter if Ric wanted college. It was a hard decision. But in the end he'd gone to school, and the old man had gotten help from the trailer court in town.

College surprised him. Ric thought he'd be fascinated with feed conversion and crop rotation theories. But he soon was liking music better. He feared his father wouldn't understand. He knew the old man would never let someone else farm "Martha's farm," as he called it.

Then Ric met Pat, just before Christmas. And that changed everything. Almost. Something about the two of them never quite made peace. It kept running on ahead, always eluding them. Pat called it poetry. He called it dissonance.

The scent of alfalfa pulled him back to the present. He left the car and walked toward the wagon, digging his fingers deep into the leafy stubble.

"By God," he said, "this is my land."

But he must go. The old man would be waiting. He saw the lilacs in the half light of the silo silhouette as he crossed the lawn. He stopped to stare at the delicate flowers. He wished his mother would be here. Pat would have learned to like the old man if she'd met him while Martha was yet alive. Pat wouldn't have called him a sloppy, clumsy peasant if she'd known the lady whose death had taken the heart from the old man. But life had chosen its own sequence of events.

He entered the sprawling house by the kitchen screen-door. The lamp beside the telephone threw gloomy shadows across the dirty floor. The sink stacked with unwashed dishes. A broken coffee cup lay upside down on the faded tablecloth.

Ric looked around for the old man. He checked the dining room and found the door ajar. He smelled cigar smoke and followed it out to the porch.

From the lawn chair in the corner the old man cleared his throat. He stood slowly to his feet and walked in silence toward his son. His hand was warm, his eyes were sad. He hadn't shaved his dreary-looking beard for weeks. Standing in the moonlight he looked like a stranger to Ric.

Without a word they turned and walked down the steps, across the terrace, and on down to the arbor by the creek. It was the favorite spot where Martha used to knit when the day's work was done and the old man would sit and smoke and talk with her. Ric remembered Pat had liked it too. He'd found her here with her guitar more than once.

The moonlight sparkled friendly in the waters of the creek as they stood there, each waiting for the other to speak. Ric wondered how the old man would accept his decision to quit college and farm. He hardly believed it himself but it was really the only choice he had. Sure, he liked the girl. But the old man had written several weeks ago and said the real estate firm was offering nearly fifteen times what he'd originally paid for the farm. Ric knew it would kill the old man if he didn't go home. The old man didn't want money. He didn't want houses on every corner of the farm. He wanted a son.

Ric remembered his decision to bring Pat here to see how she liked it. Maybe she could finish college later. Maybe the two of them could work the farm together.

But she hated it before she ever came. She said she'd rather live alone in the middle of the sea than cook for the old man until he died and left the farm to Ric and her.

He knew the old man wanted him to be happy. When Ric had left to take Pat back to the city, the old man had said Ric should go back to college if music was what he really wanted. Ric knew that meant the old man would till the soil himself until he died.

The old man spat. "How's Patricia?" he asked.

They watched the water for a moment.

"There is no more Patricia," Ric said.

The old man started. He turned stubby beard and cigar into his son's face and stared with troubled eyes. He grabbed Ric's shoulders and shook him hard. Again and again. His breath was short and quick. He leaned forward until his beard touched Ric's nose. Then he loosened his grip and turned abruptly toward the creek, throwing his cigar into the quiet waters, his face emotionless in the tranquil shadows.

"There is no more Patricia," the old man said, "and there is no more farm. I signed the papers this afternoon."

THE TENT

By Melvin Lehman

THEY THREW the last sheaf on the loaded wagon and re-treated to the shade tree at the top of the hill. Ben jabbed his pitchfork into the ground and sat down on the cool grass at the bottom of the tree.

The wagon moved slowly across the wheat stubble to the rutted patch leading down to the threshing machine. The big golden stack of wheat on the wagon shook irregularly, almost like a glob of jelly, he'd often thought, as the wheels crossed the ruts, looking for their own. Then there was the rasping sound of steel wheels against gravel and the slow, steady trot of the mules and the lazy, short-lived trails of dust as the wagon headed down the hill.

No one said anything for a while. Except for the fading sound of the wagon there was only breathing and silence.

106

Finally Aaron spoke. "If this keeps up, we'll have to get a combine next season. This is the second time already this morning the thresher broke down. We can't keep fixing up this old crate forever."

He didn't look at anyone when he talked, but Ben was sure Aaron was waiting for him to answer. They had been best friends for as long as Ben could remember. The other two men in the crew were older and married. The older men didn't like to talk about change, even change as inevitable as this, with the young unmarried men.

But one of them, Isaac Ebersole, spoke. "They said the first time this morning was only a sheared pin at the drive wheel and this time from here looks like a torn belt. Should be going any minute now."

"But yesterday morning the feeder broke down and it took all day to fix," Ben said. "It's getting harder than ever to get parts, since they don't make threshers anymore. If it rains soon, the wheat'll rot."

Isaac looked down at the thresher and pulled his right suspender back into place on his shoulder. "Well, nobody said it's easy to be an Amishman," he said. "I guess that's just part of the price we have to pay to be different from the world."

Ben looked over at Aaron and saw him in profile — the wavy hair, the intelligent eyes, the slightly large nose, and the mouth which was either laughing or serious, usually not much in between.

"But how will getting a combine make us worldly?" Aaron asked.

MOST OF THE men beside the thresher were stepping away now, and Ben saw his father and another man walking up to the tractor.

The fourth man, Eli Beiler, hadn't said anything so far. He had kept quiet and watched the others as they talked. He was a thin man with gray hair.

Now he began speaking, not looking at anyone in particular as he spoke. "That's what I thought when I was your age. I thought, What's the harm in trying a little something new for a change?" He chose his words carefully. Somehow Ben knew the argument was over now. "What's wrong with radios? I said. What's wrong with cars? But when you get as old as me, you'll see it just doesn't work that way. If we start using combines, pretty soon we'd be using cars, and then we'd get electricity and radios and television. Before you know it, you young men would be going to high school and college and getting worldly ideas, and the girls would cut their hair and use lipstick and go to dances."

He was clearly just getting warmed up — there was no telling how long he could have gone on when they heard the tractor kick into life at the bottom of the hill. One of the men was giving the belt a final tug, and then he stepped back and shouted to the man on the tractor — the first sound from the men Ben had heard all morning. The men stood still as the old thresher wound itself up to operating speed. Then threshing began again in earnest.

Eli had been right, Ben knew. There were no two ways about it. If they bought a combine, if they started acting like the world, no telling where they'd end up. Pop said the Mennonites hadn't been much different from them not too many years ago, but they'd started getting cars and radios and going to high school and college and now you could hardly tell their young people from the world. You just couldn't argue with facts like those.

The world, at least from everything he'd seen and read

about it in the Lancaster newspapers, really wasn't too good a place. He'd read all about the riots in the big cities. Why do people act that way, anyhow? he wondered. And so what if they were winning the war in Vietnam? It seemed they sure had to kill a lot of people to do it.

No, he could never quite figure out the world. The world was where people murdered each other and got divorced and went on strikes. The world was where people got education and thought they were smart. They were often the stuck-up kind who came driving around in big cars. The world was where LSD was in one year and meditation with the guru or whatever the next. The world was where people shot each other. Maybe the Amish couldn't figure out exactly what all Robert Kennedy was saying, but they certainly wouldn't have shot him. The world was where women walked around the streets half-naked in the summertime.

The wagon at the tresher was almost unloaded and Ben's little brother, Timothy, was already walking toward it. He tried to find the right word to describe the Amish in contrast to the rest of the world. It wasn't simply "different" or "plain." No, not even just "rural" or "farmers." He looked over the farmland again. Around him in the distance he could see at least three other crews threshing wheat this morning. The right word was almost on the tip of his tongue when he saw it, and immediately he wished he'd have kept looking at the thresher.

"Every time!" he said to himself. "Every time!" Just when he was beginning to have all the answers, when he was feeling the happiest, he either thought about it, or, like now, actually saw it — the tent. He dug his heels into the ground and pushed himself up an inch higher along the tree trunk.

He shouldn't have been surprised at all about seeing the tent from this hill, but it was way over near Paradise along the Lincoln Highway, and if he had been down in the valley with the other men, he wouldn't have been able to see it. He'd seen it close up before, but even at this distance it was decidedly ugly. It was low, yellowish brown, and fat, with the canvas roof sagging down from the top. It bordered on the ridiculous. All around it were golden wheat and green cornfields and there, plop in the middle, was the ridiculously stupid, ugly tent.

Ben looked over at Aaron, and when Aaron turned and glanced at Ben, they realized they both had been staring at it. Ben opened his mouth to start to speak; but Aaron jerked his head in the direction of the older men, and neither of them said anything.

Down at the thresher, Timothy climbed on the wagon and the mules began moving. The morning sun was beginning to feel hot, even in the shade. Ben wondered whether his brother would bring a can of water along on the wagon.

He was about to open his shoelaces when he heard the car coming on the road behind him. He didn't bother to turn around and he wouldn't have, either, except that when it reached the tree, it stopped. He took a deep breath. Tourists.

THEY TURNED around slowly. Ben was glad Eli and Isaac were with him; somehow tourists made him nervous. The car was a 1968 Oldsmobile, he knew from reading newspaper advertisements. It was long, low, and silvery blue. The windshield was tinted blue at the top. He looked at the license plate: orange lettering on a dark blue background. New York. He'd seen this kind of people before.

The driver's door was opening, and a big, fleshly man

was slowly climbing out. The back door on the driver's side flew open and a little boy, close to Timothy's age, leaped out. As soon as he saw Ben and the others, he pointed at them and began jumping up and down, "Look, Mommy," he yelled. "Real, live Amishmen!" The man didn't look at him, but he began smiling.

The others were getting out on the far side of the car now. The little boy reached into the car and pulled out a camera. He began taking pictures of them, of the country-side, of his dad, of the sky — everything. Ben's family didn't own a camera themselves, because the church was against it. But from the price of film and developing he'd seen in the stores, he figured pictures were pretty expensive.

The mother and the two daughters from the other side had come around the car now. The little boy was still taking pictures. The mother smiled and tapped him on the shoulder. "Brian," she said, "would you please stop taking so many pictures?" Ben wasn't sure whether to feel amusement or contempt. When his mother wanted Timothy to stop doing something, she just told him to stop it and that was that. "Would you please." Imagine!

The tourist family all stood together beside the car a moment. Then they began walking toward the Amish. Ben couldn't be sure of the age of the wife. It was hard to tell how old worldly women were, especially rich, worldly women. The other daughter was little, maybe a twin to Brian. Ben noticed the two girls and the mother were all wearing the same colored shorts — red and blue plaid. Amazing! He —

The father was speaking. "Well, you're taking a break now, boys?" He smiled broadly, a little too broadly, Ben thought. Ben and Aaron stood up first, and the two older men followed. For a few seconds no one said anything. Then Eli spoke. "The thresher broke down for about ten minutes and we had to wait while they fixed it."

"The what broke down?" the man asked, wrinkling his forehead, but still smiling. Ben looked at him. He saw now he wasn't a particularly big man after all, but his stomach was huge, his belt marking an equator across it. His lips and lower jaw were fleshy.

"Mommy, ask them if I can get a buggy ride," Brian pleaded, tugging on his mother's arm. Everyone except the Amish completely ignored him.

"The thresher broke down," Eli repeated. "We use it to thresh the wheat." He nodded in the direction of the valley.

The tourists turned. "Good grief, look at that thing!" the wife said, lifting her hand halfway to her mouth. "May we see it close up?" she asked.

"Oh, I guess so," Aaron agreed, shrugging. Eli and Isaac looked at him sharply. When Aaron saw them, he turned slowly toward the valley.

Ben watched his brother driving the mules up toward him. The mules were still moving at the same speed. For once he wished they would move faster.

Brian was taking pictures again. "Look at those men — they're all working," the New York man said. "I read a book about your people before we came down here to Lancaster County. Hex signs — the works. I read it all. But what I can't figure out is, how do you keep them all working? You don't have any bosses, do you, and they don't get paid?"

Isaac simply shrugged his shoulders, but Eli said, "That's just the way we do it — harvesttime we all get together and work. We all just work."

The man was still smiling. He took a deep breath and let it out through his mouth. "My, it must be great living out here, isn't it? No smog, no congestion, no murders or riots, no strikes, no noise." He was obviously beginning to get carried away. "You people just don't know how — "

"Do your people get married?" the wife asked. "I thought I read somewhere that none of you get married — you all stay single and live in little houses or something. Is that true?"

Eli shook his head seriously. "No, we get married. Isaac and I are married, but Ben and Aaron here, aren't yet."

Ben turned around and saw Timothy was halfway to them by now. "Do you have a girl friend?" he heard someone ask. He turned around slowly and suddenly realized the older daughter was looking directly at him. Oh, no, he thought. Why did God make mules so blame slow?

He looked at the ground. He had to say something. He couldn't just stand there like an idiot; but whatever happened he was sure of one thing — he wasn't going to bring Sarah into this.

"Yeah," he said.

"Is she pretty?" the girl asked, smiling. For the first time, Ben looked directly at her. She had long blond hair curling at her shoulders. Ben thought he remembered vaguely thinking once that he didn't like blond girls and now he was sure. For some reason, he suddenly wondered if New York City girls ever blushed.

Ben didn't answer right away.

"Well, maybe we better get back to work," Ben heard Eli say. "The wagon's — "

"Oh, but of course she's pretty," the mother said, smiling, but keeping her lips pressed together. "What would you expect with a big, strong farm boy like him!" The mother and daughter looked at each other and smiled.

"Hey, could we get a picture of you guys before you go back to work?" the man asked. "Like all of you hold your forks in front of you and smile, or something."

Eli glanced at Isaac and then he spoke. "Mister, we wouldn't mind, but our church doesn't allow it, so I guess we better not."

"Oh, come on," the tourist said. "Only one won't matter, will it? Just one picture, huh?"

"What do you think?" Isaac said to the other three in Pennsylvania Dutch. "Maybe that way we can get rid of them. There's no telling how long they'll stay."

"The boy already took some," Aaron said.

"We can't *let* him take it," Eli said. "It's against church rules. You can't just go — "

They heard a click. The man had taken the camera from Brian and snapped a picture. As they looked up at him, he laughed and took another.

"There, that wasn't so bad, was it now?" he said, smiling more than ever. "I can't begin to thank you fellows enough. Well, we'll have to go and let you good men work." He reached into his pocket. "Here, take this," he said, pulling out a half-dollar. He walked over and gave it to Ben. "Buy something for your girl friend with this." He winked. "Be good now." They walked back to the car and started getting in. "Good-bye," they all said and waved. Ben saw the blond-haired girl looking at him and smiling. He tried his best to return the smile but he could only grin weakly. They were all still waving and smiling as the car drove out of sight.

He turned the half-dollar over in his hand carefully —

1967, almost brand-new, silver, and shiny. He looked at
the edge. Yes, it was like all the new ones these days —
three layers, two shiny ones on the outside and a dull
copper one in the middle. They didn't even try to cover the
center layer up. There it was, easy to see if you took the
time to look closely.

He glanced toward the threshing machine and then he
saw it again — the tent. Every time! Why did it have to
be every time? He turned his back to the thresher and
faced the other side of the hill. It had been a long time
since he'd skipped flat stones on the creek and he wondered if he could still do it. He pinched the coin edge-
ways between his thumb and index finger so hard that it
hurt. He took a deep breath, drew his arm back, and then
threw it with all his might.

It was a beautiful throw, rising slightly and then slowly
dropping to the ground. He'd never thrown anything so
far before in his life. Finally it landed somewhere in the
corn patch his neighbor Amos Stoltzfus owned. It was
lost now, but sometime, ten or twenty years from now,
somebody would be plowing some spring and see it and
wonder how in the world a 1967 half-dollar ever got in
the middle of the field.

He would have looked longer, but Timothy arrived
with the mules and wagon.

HE THOUGHT, for a moment, of holding her hand, but
somehow, this didn't seem the right time or place. So
far, neither of them had spoken, but it seemed to him
that Sarah was the one who wasn't talking. Ben glanced
over at her. She was looking down at the road. No matter
how hot it was, she always appeared composed and cool.

There was something special about a summer evening,

he thought. It was just about the best time he could think of. Working all day in the hot sun had a way of draining your energy, tightening your nerves a little, but in the evening you knew it was all worth it.

He wished one of them would say something. He thought of complimenting her on the cookies she made for the evening treat, but since he knew it was Sarah who wasn't talking, he decided to wait for her. The moon was just becoming bright over the corn tassles ahead to their right when she spoke.

"Are you still going to do it, Ben?" she asked.

He kicked a stone lying on the road and watched it skid into the weeds along the side. "Look, I was hoping I could talk to you alone sometime this week," he said. "There were too many people around yesterday after church and I couldn't explain myself right. I don't think I made it clear enough." He looked over at her. "You didn't tell anybody, did you?"

She looked up at him. Her eyes were brown and large in the near-darkness. "No," she said, "you told me not to, so I didn't."

He nodded and paused. "Well, let me start at the beginning. It's almost two years now since they first set up the tent over near Paradise. They have this big sign out front, well, you saw it yourself. It says, '*A Funny Thing Happened to Me on My Way to the Hoedown*, now playing.' We figured it was just another tourist trap — there's all kinds of them along the Lincoln Highway.

"Then last Saturday night me and Aaron didn't have anything else to do so we decided, just for the fun of it, to stop in. It was almost eight when we got there. We didn't have much money so we both bought the cheapest tickets they had, two bucks each. Before the clerk handed us our tickets, she stepped out of the booth and whispered to one of the ushers. When we handed him our tickets, he took us right up to the second or third row. That ain't normal, is it?

"When we walked up — I can't describe it exactly — but we could just feel everyone's eyes on us, you know? When we were walking up, I heard some fat woman say — well, I don't know whether she was fat or not, I just heard her talking — she said, 'Good gracious, Cynthia. It's some of them.' Some man, up farther on the other side of the aisle, said in a deep cigarette-voice. 'Hey, look at that, Charlie. You think they're the real thing or just part of the show? Was I ever glad when we sat down!

"It wasn't long before the play started. There was this New York psychologist or sociologist or something who came down to study us Amish. While he was down he stayed with an Amish family. The whole way through, the Amish did stupid stuff — tripping over wheelbarrows and spilling paint over hex signs. The tourists laughed and laughed. The New York man was always calm and cool. The tourists never laughed at him."

Ben glanced over at her and saw that she was looking directly at him. The moon lit up only the left side of her face and she appeared even more beautiful than before. He looked down at the road. Wondering how long she had been looking at him made him feel funny inside.

He began again. "While he was down here, this New York guy and the Amish girl — she had dark-brown hair like you — were alone together one evening and the Amish girl, Katie, I think her name was, let him kiss her. Sarah, you know that just wouldn't happen. Amish girls have more principle than that. I didn't remember much else of the play, except that they didn't get married. Can't you see,

Sarah, they treated us like children! They laughed at us! As soon as it was over, Aaron and I cleared out of there as fast as we could."

Sarah was looking at the ground now. She wrinkled her forehead slightly. "Well, why not let it go at that, then?" she asked. "They laugh at us, they think we're stupid, but we know we're right. And we're happy. That's the important thing, isn't it?"

He both loved her and hated her for disagreeing. "Look, Sarah, you're hardly ever around when the tourists stop and talk to us," he said. "You're always in the house, shelling beans, or something. It's always the same. They're rich, slick, smiling. They think they know all about us when they don't know anything. Sarah, it gets to you after a while. You know, you feel you've got to do something. Don't you see?"

She didn't say anything. He went on. "So Aaron and I started thinking. 'We've got to do something,' we said. It was Aaron's idea. Some Sunday evening when they're giving the play, we'll get about a dozen guys together. Right at the scene when the New York guy kisses the Amish girl, we'll spread out around the tent, pull out our butcher knives, or whatever we can find at home, and each cut two of the ropes holding up the sides of the tent. They aren't big ropes. With butcher knives we can easily cut two and then run away. Sarah, listen, I just thought of this now. We'll make a note, see, with something real neat written on it, and leave it close to the door. Man, I can just see it now — the sides of that old tent caving in." He was grinning now. "Isn't it beautiful?"

Sarah wasn't smiling. "But, Ben," she said, "that's not the way our people act." They turned in the lane leading to her farm. "We believe in peace. So what if the sides of

"Some Sunday evening when they're having the play, we'll take butcher knives and cut the ropes holding up the sides of the tent."

the tent collapse and you get back at the tourists? Then what? What good will it do?"

"Do you really expect me just to sit back and take all this crap from the New York city slickers?" Ben said. "We have got to let them know we're here, let them know we're real people."

"But the Bible says, 'Love your enemies,' " Sarah said. "How can you do what you're going to do and still love them?"

Ben almost raised his voice but he caught himself and spoke, he thought, calmly. "Look, we're not killing anybody. We just want to have a little fun. Nobody's going to get hurt."

She paused and then began shaking her head slowly. "But it's the spirit of the thing that's wrong, Ben. Our people just don't act that way and we've always been happy. Somehow it doesn't seem right."

He didn't answer. The rest of the way in the lane neither of them spoke.

They were standing outside her door. "Then you're against it for certain?" he asked.

She nodded silently.

"But you've got to understand, Sarah. I have to do it. You can take so much for so long and then something has to give."

The crickets were coming out now and a few firebugs flew around randomly. Except for the moon it was altogether dark. Ben met her eyes and they looked at each other. "Sarah," he said, "this won't change anything between us, will it?"

She shook her head silently, looking directly at him.

He took her hand. "Good night," he said.

"Good night," she whispered. She turned and went into the house.

THEY CLIMBED into the carriage again, the third time that afternoon, and with a flick of the reins were off. Ben waited until they were out of Pete's lane before he spoke.

"Well, so we can't get Pete. That leaves only Jonas, and we knew we could get him all along. I really wish we could have gotten Pete, though. He'd be a good guy to have along on something like this."

"Yeah, but what can you expect from a guy that's engaged," Aaron said. "Why should he risk his tail on some fly-by-night operation like this. He's got a woman to love him — it's as simple as that. Why rock the boat?"

"Then you don't believe that he meant it at all when he talked about 'Love thine enemies' and how what we're going to do is only how the world acts?"

"Of course not — he's engaged."

"Well, you have to admit he has a point," Ben said defensively. "Sarah was saying about the same thing. Maybe the thing we should try to do is to love these tourists."

"Don't be crazy," Aaron said. "After all, we're not killing anybody. Nobody's getting hurt. So far the tourists have had a thousand laughs and we haven't had any. All we're trying to do is make it one thousand to one, that's all."

Ben watched the front wheel of the buggy going around. The fast steady trot of the horses and the steel-rimmed wheels rolling on the road were somehow comforting. They went past a lane with some of the stones pushed out on the road. There was a cracky, rasping sound and the buggy swayed slightly as they hit the rocks. Then they settled back to the softly rumbling, delicately solid sound of steel-rimmed buggy wheels on the road.

"I guess I believe you," Ben finally said. "But still, I sort of — you know what I mean — *feel* something deep inside." They were passing a row of trees along the road. He watched as the sunlight flashed on and off the black polished spokes of the wheel. "Somehow, it seems this isn't the way we're supposed to act. It seems like what the world does, not us. That's just the way I feel sometimes, even if I don't want to."

Aaron was looking straight ahead at the horse. "Huh, that's where you're wrong," he said. "You can't just go around feeling all the time. Anybody can feel anything. You've got to think, not feel. I think it's obvious we're right. Look at Hitler. He certainly felt he was right, but six million Jews still died."

Ben didn't answer. To their left was the hill where they had met the tourists on Monday. A Greyhound bus had stopped now, he noticed, and a herd of tourists was filing out. It was less than a quarter of a mile away, across a field of young corn, and Ben could see them perfectly. He saw the woman tour guide gesture dramatically — for the view, he supposed. He'd observed more than his share of snooty-faced tour guides, he thought, with their lily-white hands and stupid-sweet smiles. While he was watching, the tour guide pointed down at them. Some of the tourists had noticed them and were lifting their cameras.

Ben turned to Aaron. "You're right," he said, gritting his teeth. "You've got to be right because this Sunday night that old tent's comin' down."

"Atta boy," Aaron grinned, and patted him on the shoulder. "I knew you'd pull through."

Comin' down. Coming down. "Comin' down" definitely was the better choice, Ben thought. It sounded better somehow.

He was still thinking about it when they passed Sarah's farm. She was out picking raspberries. She was stooping over, but when she saw them coming she stood up, waved, and started running across the potato rows toward them. "Ben, wait!" she called. When she got to them she was out of breath and smiling. A lock of brown hair had fallen across her forehead. "Did you hear about the singing they're having at Fishers this Sunday night?" she asked. She pushed the strand of hair back into place. "It's going to be an extra big one. Are you coming?"

Ben looked at Aaron. "Oh, I guess I could meet you there around ten-thirty or eleven."

"But, Ben," she said, looking directly at him, "they told me they want you to sing and play your guitar. Couldn't you make it any earlier?" she asked hopefully.

"I'm sorry, Sarah," he said firmly, "but I'm afraid it just won't suit that early." He could see the hurt in her eyes now. He could tell she hadn't forgotten about the tent.

"Look, we've got to get going," Aaron said. "It's not too long until milking time, and we still haven't talked to Jonas yet." The horses had already begun to move. Ben was still looking back. "So long," he said, and tried to smile.

Sarah just stood there smiling faintly. Ben turned around. Jonas' house was only a half mile away.

JONAS AND Davy and Reuben and the rest of them were all there, talking and laughing softly. Aaron and Ben sat over to the side by themselves. They hadn't talked much.

"Couldn't have picked a better night if we'd tried," Aaron said. "Can't hardly see a thing."

Ben looked up. Except for a few scattered patches of

gray, the sky was black. The moon hadn't shown through all evening. "Yeah," he said.

They watched the lights from the tent just on the other side of the hill. They could hear the band when it played and the occasional laughter and applause, but it was at least an hour since the cars had parked and the chatter of the tourists had floated over the hill to them.

Ben heard the sheaves of wheat rustle beside him. "I guess it's about that time," Aaron said to him, and then got up and walked over to where the others were sitting. Ben stayed where he was.

Reuben was the first to see him coming. "Aha," he said, "we're goin' now."

"Listen," Aaron said. "This'll be the last time I go over this, so let's get everything straight. If you have any questions, ask them now."

They listened closely as Aaron told them exactly how they would wait for the song, "Your Eyes Have Put a Hex on Me," how they would spread out on the way down, how they would cut the ropes, and how they would leave the note at the door.

"You have the note, don't you, Ben?" Aaron asked.

"Yeah," Ben said, and held it up.

"We can't read it from here," someone said. "What's it say?"

"It's a poster advertising this play," Aaron said. "The back says, 'A Funny Thing Happened to Some New York City Slickers While They Were Visiting the Plain People.' "

They all laughed. "Hey, not bad," Davy said.

"Did you sign it?" someone else asked.

"Oh, I forgot about that," Aaron said. "Does anybody have a pencil real quick?" A few of the boys rummaged through their pockets.

"We head up through the cornfield, then?" asked Reuben.

"Yeah," Aaron said, "the girls are waiting on the other side. They'll take us to the singing. Just don't get lost in the corn."

"Don't worry," Davy said. "If we know there's girls waiting on the other side we won't get lost." They laughed again.

Someone had produced a pencil. "Here, Aaron, you sign first," Reuben said.

Ben saw Aaron lean over, in the stillness he could hear the pencil. "Everybody just sign their first name. That way they can't prove anything on us if there's any trouble."

There was a brief silence. "What do you mean, 'trouble'?" Jonas asked.

Aaron had already started toward the tent. He turned around. "Who knows, this may even make the Lancaster newspapers. If it does, we'll clip it out and save it to show to our grandchildren." He could always think of something funny to say.

Ben could vaguely see the others signing it now, talking and chuckling as they did. Well, after all, he said to himself, sometimes a man has to just make a decision and say this is what he's going to do and then do it. So what if Sarah and Pete both disagreed with him? Since when did those two alone have a corner on all the wisdom and truth in the world?

He heard a sudden burst of laughter from the tent, swallowed up by applause. Pete even said he would have done it himself when he was their age, but not now. What could you expect from a guy getting married in a couple months? And Sarah was always in the house working when the tourists came. You had to see the New Yorkers firsthand to know what they were really like.

Reuben was walking over with the poster, "Now you sign it," he said. Ben bent down and looked. All the other fellows had signed. He took the pencil and began printing his name very carefully. B-E-N. Ben.

He crawled to the top of the hill and looked for Aaron. When they saw each other, Aaron waved. The get-ready signal. Ben turned around and told the boys. Someone mentioned the knives. The moon was still hidden, but Ben thought he saw faint glimmerings of steel as the boys pulled out their knives for a final inspection. At the most, Ben figured, they'd have four or five minutes.

If there was any one reason why he disliked the New Yorkers most, he thought, it was that they thought they knew everything and they really didn't know anything — like the hex sign business, for instance.

In fact, there were all kinds of things they didn't know about, he mused. They didn't know anything about watching Pop cut a big piece of still-warm shoofly pie and pour chilled applesauce on top. Mom would watch as Pop frowned slightly when he took the first bite and chewed it thoughtfully. Then he'd look over at her and smile and she'd blush and look down and begin eating hers.

The New Yorkers didn't know about everybody sitting around on Sunday afternoon after church was over and staying until just before milking time. The men would talk about farming, the women about housekeeping, and the young people about almost anything.

The tourists didn't know working hard all day long on a patch of corn and turning around to look back at the fresh brown dirt before going home to supper.

They didn't know about riding home from Sunday evening singing very slowly in your buggy with corn and

wheat on both sides of the road, a big full moon overhead, and holding hands with your girl — not saying anything, just holding hands.

They didn't know watching Pop slowly, thoughtfully open
the family Bible to read before the evening meal and knowing, as you watched him read, that he was at peace with
his God.

No, the New Yorkers didn't know any of this. They came
in their big cars, they pointed, they laughed, they took
pictures, and they thought they knew everything. Then they
went back to New York and drank beer or watched TV or
read dirty books or whatever it was New Yorkers did.

He wasn't quite sure, but he knew they didn't do what
Amish did. They left and thought they knew everything. It
was almost as if they were — he tried to find the right
word — half-wits.

The word caught him hard. He hadn't thought of it
quite like that before. He had a second cousin who was a
half-wit. Pop had always said to be extra kind to him, never
to tease him or make fun of him. The funny thing was,
his second cousin always thought he was normal; he never
seemed to know he was mixed up.

Ben looked down at Aaron, but Aaron was still watching
the tent. He wished Aaron would hurry up. The rest of
the fellows weren't talking much now, but he thought he
could see they were still polishing their knives. He looked
up at the sky. It was still dark, with only here and there a
patch of light visible.

While he was on the subject, he thought, there was just
one other thing he had to get straight. Sarah and Pete had
both said that this wasn't the way their people acted. The
world was where people fought and killed, but Amish believed in peace and love. Sure, Aaron would say they

weren't killing anybody, but somehow, what they were doing just didn't seem in the spirit of his people.

Suddenly the crash of cymbals and a fluttering of violins shattered the still night air, and the band started up again. Ben wished he had a few hours by himself to think this thing through. What was the matter with him, anyway? Once Aaron made up his mind, he stuck to it. He looked down at Aaron again. He still had his back turned; but then, as Ben watched, he turned around and beckoned with his hand. Ben felt strangely weary as he turned to signal the group.

IT HAPPENED so fast Ben could hardly understand his feelings. They had been individuals before, but suddenly they could see everybody else; for the first time all evening, the moon burst out from behind the clouds. They were entranced. It was as if they really hadn't seen each other at all before. Everyone was standing now in a loose circle with their black pants and vests.

It was the knives. Most of them were long and glittering in the moonlight. The boys looked around the group from faces to knives. They looked at their own knives carefully and turned them over slowly.

"Aaron says for us to get going," Ben said vaguely, but he wasn't at all surprised when no one moved. There certainly| were a lot of different-shaped knives, he noticed. There was the standard butcher knife with the straight back and slowly tapering blade with the heel sticking out near the handle. Some of the knives were newer with small, smooth teeth at the bottom. Ben's mother used them for cutting bread when it was soft. One or two knives were short and thick, but sharpened so long the cutting edge was worn almost to the back. Some of the boys were running their thumbs and index fingers along the side of the knives, and occasionally touching the sharp edge with their fingers. They looked down at their fingers, almost surprised not to see blood.

No matter how a knife was held, Ben noticed, it looked evil, wicked. Holding it with the blade toward the little finger made you think of a hard stab down the neck or into the rib cage. Holding it with the blade toward your thumb made you think of a quick, slashing drive up through the belly and into the diaphragm.

Ben forced his mind back to the task at hand. Aaron would probably be furious by now, he thought. Ben moved toward the group and for the first time, they looked at him. Telling them to get going seemed ridiculous now. He glanced over at the lights from the tent. "Look," he said, and suddenly the whole idea came to him. "I was just thinking about something. You know how city slickers are. If the sides of the tent cave in, they might all panic and start running around and suffocating or something. Maybe we ought to call this whole thing off."

He watched the group as the idea began to sink in. Some of them were still looking at their knives. Others were looking at the ground or staring into the distance. Nobody looked directly at anybody else. A few of them began smiling weakly. "Yeah," someone said, "there's no telling what those New York women might do. They'd probably go crazy, screaming and all."

Aaron came running over the hill. "Hey, what's the holdup?" he said. "They'll be kissing any — "

The group was slowly breaking up. Most of them began drifting toward the road that led around the cornfield to where the girls were waiting.

"Wait," Aaron called.

"They'll all suffocate," someone said. Most of the others only turned around and looked.

Aaron turned on Ben angrily. "What the world's going on?" he said furiously in a hoarse whisper. "What happened?"

All the rest were walking away now. Ben suddenly realized he had to do all the explaining himself, but he knew he couldn't. The magic of the moment was gone. Already the moon had gone behind the clouds and it was dark. He could only try.

"We all were ready to go when you gave the signal," Ben said. "Just then the moon came out, remember? For the first time we saw all of us together with our knives."

"What's so great about that?" Aaron said. "Everybody saw his knife this afternoon."

"It was different this time, though, seeing all our knives at once. We just stood there and looked. So I said if we cut the ropes, everybody might suffocate. They all agreed and then everybody started leaving."

Aaron stared at him in disbelief. "But we went over that before, soon after we got the idea. Don't you remember? The top of the tent is still held up by poles and chains. Just the sides will fall in a bit — a little excitement, that's all. Don't you remember?"

Ben looked at the ground, nodding silently.

"Then why did you say it?" Aaron asked furiously. He wasn't whispering anymore. "We were planning this thing for a whole week. Why in the world did you all of a sudden decide to blow it?"

Ben looked down at his knife. He wondered how he would tell Sarah about it. If he knew Sarah, she would smile when he went to meet her, but she wouldn't ask any questions. Later, when they were alone, she would wait, and then he'd explain the whole thing from the beginning, or at least tell what happened.

He finally looked up at Aaron. "I don't know," he said. "I'm not sure." There was another crash of cymbals from the tent, and what he thought were trumpets started out in unison and then harmonized. He ran his finger delicately along the cutting edge of the knife. "But I promise you one thing," he said, "when I do figure it all out, you'll be the first person I tell."

THE TIGER OF SAMARKAND

By Kenneth Reed

SMALL BOYS are thought to be too playful to understand the Book of Revelation. It isn't true.

Hermann and David, for example, understood perfectly the millennium and the second coming of Jesus Christ, and they were only twelve. Well, not actually. Hermann wasn't quite twelve yet, but he understood "future things" better than David. David was more interested in tigers.

"How long will it be yet until Jesus comes?" asked David. "It's getting awfully hot; will He wait until fall?"

"A month or two, I'm not sure which."

"Who said?"

"The prophet."

"I don't believe it; that's what he said last year," said David.

"But that was before the comet. He'll tell us tonight, if we ask him."

"True. Hermann."

"What?"

"My tan's better than yours."

"I always have to ride in the wagon. It ain't fair."

"Papa says we'll all be black by the time Jesus comes. Hermann."

"What?"

"I don't believe Jesus is going to come."

"Take it back."

"It's the truth."

"Take it back."

"No."

"Take it back or I'll put sand in your mouth." He grabbed David by the leg and pulled back as David dived forward. They went down together onto the hot sand. They rolled over and over, a whirl of white cloth and dark legs on the white sand. Hermann had him.

"Now, say you believe or I'll put this," he held a handful of sand high overhead, "in your mouth." Some trickled out and fell on David's tongue. He began to cough.

"Quit faking."

But the boy's eyes rolled upward and his stomach heaved. He began to pant.

"David. David. Are you okay? David!" Hermann shook his shoulders. He stood up and began to run, panic-stricken, and suddenly he fell down on his face.

"Now, I'm on top."

"Oh, don't bounce on me, David. Don't bounce on me, please. That's not fair. You pretended a lie, and no liar will go up to meet Jesus . . . ohh . . . when He comes."

"He's not coming."

"Don't tell a lie."

"He's not."

"Claas Epp said He is."

"It's not true. He's crazy."

"David!"

"Say he's crazy or I'll fill up your ears with sand."

"No, don't. You could ruin my ears. That's not fair. You can spit it out of your mouth but you can't spit it out of your ears."

"Hurry up, say it."

"It isn't true."

"Okay, then we start with one grain."

"Ohh . . ."

"And another one. This is taking too long. Two more . . ."

"Stop, I'll say it, I'll say it."

"Okay."

"But it won't be true, even if I say it, and you know it. He's our leader appointed by God to take us to the place of refuge. Do you want to say that God is crazy? Huh?"

"Two more in this ear . . ."

"David, they tickle. I think my ear . . ."

"Well, hurry up and say he's crazy then."

"Okay, he's crazy."

"Who's crazy? You have to say who."

"Claas."

"Which Claas? Maybe you mean my brother Claas. How dare you?"

"Stop bouncing on me. I'll say it."

"Quick, because I'm going to put fifty grains in this time."

"Claas Epp is crazy."

"Okay. Did you hear that, Moon?"

"Oh, my back aches. Look. I can't even touch my toes."

"You never could."

"Yes I could." Suddenly Hermann's bare feet flashed and a spray of sand flew up in David's face. "There, I still say he's not crazy." And he began to run.

"Hermann, if you don't come back I'll tell your father what you said." Hermann came back. "Brush the sand off my robe, or I still might tell."

"Boy, you must think I'm your slave."

"Yes, you are my slave, just like the sultan of Samarkand. Kiss my toe, oh slave."

"Sultan."

"Yes, slave."

"I . . ."

"You will be quiet until the Sultan has spoken."

"But David . . ."

"SULTAN!"

"Yes, Sultan."

"We are going to proceed west for another week until we find the Amu Darya River. There we will plant grapevines and fig trees and wait for Jesus to come and begin His thousand-year reign on earth." David stood up and shook the sand from his white robe majestically. He stretched out his arm and made a quick fist, so hard that his knuckles turned white. "My people! My people, we have traveled . . . as pilgrims and strangers . . ." He looked down from the corner of his eye at the slave, who was picking at his ear. "We have traveled as pilgrims and strangers . . ."

"You said that before."

"Silence."

"Why do I have to keep silent and listen to you? You don't say it nearly as good as Brother Epp does anyway."

"Brother Epp? Don't mention that man to the Sultan or you will lose your head."

"Well, it's his speech you're giving."

"No, it's not."

"It sounds like it to me."

"You haven't heard the end yet."

"Hurry up, David. I'm getting hungry."

"David? Who's he?"

"Okay."

"Not okay. 'Yes, Sultan!' "

"I'm not saying it anymore."

"All right, so I tell your father that you said Claas Epp was crazy. He will tell Mr. Epp. And Mr. Epp will put the mark of the beast on your forehead and leave you on the desert for the devil."

"You made me say he was crazy. You put sand in my ear and now I can't get it out."

David drew himself into the figure of the prophet again.

"We have traveled as pilgrims and strangers from our homes in Russia for two long 'tribulous' years in search of the place of refuge. And now, O God, You have revealed to Your prophet Elijah and to Your people the church of Philipia . . ."

"Philadelphia."

"The church of Philadelphia spoken of in the vision to Saint John as he lay without hope on the isle of Patmos, even as we lay without hope in the prison of our homes in Russia . . . You have spoken, O Sultan, to your slaves, of the place of refuge in the east when Jesus Christ will come to meet His saints, amen, and now we have come."

"Ha, ha."

"What's wrong?"

"You said, 'You have spoken, O Sultan, to your slaves, of the place of refuge.' "

"What difference does it make who spoke? God moves in a mysterious way, His wonders to perform."

"You really sound like *him*, David."

"Of course, I am him."

"I thought you were the Sultan."

"I am Claas Epp, the prophet, and also the Sultan."

"That's impossible."

"All things are possible with God."

"Claas Epp argued with the Sultan of Samarkand. That's why we have a guard, stupid. To protect us from the Sultan's spies. You can't be both the Sultan and Claas Epp. They're opposites. Like fire and water."

"I am fire and water to my people. I am firewater from God."

"You're crazy."

"What?"

"I said you're crazy."

"You called the prophet of God crazy? God will strike you down. Strike him down, God."

"I'm still alive."

"Look. Look. A comet."

"There's always a comet at night."

"That comet is God's fire coming to get you. God's fire that is hotter than — hotter than a campfire . . . hotter than this desert . . . so hot that the world will go 'poof.' And that fire is coming to get you."

"No, no."

"See it coming. Repent!"

"I didn't mean it."

"Repent!"

"I'm sorry."

"About what? God's fire is coming, see. See it. Will it strike this time? Ohh . . . Ohh . . ."

"No, don't strike me."

"Repent!"

"I'm sorry I said you were crazy."

"Who am I?"

"You are the prophet."

"Ah, brother, God has spared you. See, the fire is disappearing."

"Yes."

"Jesus is speaking to me."

"Yes."

"He is saying, 'Push on, My faithful ones.' "

"Yes."

" 'You are nearing the place of refuge, where I will come again to get My people.' "

"Yes."

" 'And then I will burn up the world with My fire . . . poof!' "

"Yes."

" 'Build yourselves homes on the Amu Darya River and plant grapes and figs.' "

"But we don't know how to raise figs."

" 'I will show you.' "

"Yes."

" 'And when the fig tree blossoms and the grapevine has grapes, you and your family will sit under them. . . .' "

"Yes, Jesus."

" 'And wait for Me to come, because as I have promised in the prophet Micah, in the last days every man will sit under his vine and under his fig tree. The last days are here. I am coming very soon.' "

"It must be gooey."

"What?"

"Sitting under a grapevine. Rotten grapes are always falling off."

"Are you saying you don't want to sit under a grapevine?"

"I don't know," said Hermann.

"You don't want to meet Jesus when He comes?"

"No, I didn't mean that."

"Then you will sit under a grapevine. Now . . ."

"David."

"Who?"

"David, I'm tired of playing this."

"Playing? Who's playing? I am the prophet."

"David, look. Here he comes."

"Who?"

"It's Claas Epp."

"And my father and all the people," said David.

"They're singing, David. *Befiel du deine Wege.* And they're wearing their white robes."

"It must be time."

"Maybe tonight he will really tell us."

"Tell us what?"

"When Jesus is coming."

"Hermann."

"What?"

"Hermann. I don't believe it."

"What?"

"I don't believe Claas Epp knows when Jesus is coming."

"You mean you think he's a liar?"

"I don't know. I don't believe him!"

"David!"

"I don't want to go to heaven," said David.

"God will strike you dead for saying that. . . ."

"I just want to lie here and look at the stars and think about the tiger we saw in Samarkand."

"The Tiger of Samarkand" is based on a true story. In the early 1900s Claas Epp led a group of Mennonites in a wild trek across Russia in search of "a place of refuge" where Jesus would meet them in His second coming. The trek lasted four years, with Epp getting progressively more fanatical, seeing himself first as Elijah and finally as Jesus Christ Himself. The group was harassed by Russian Arabs and finally disbanded about the time they reached the Amu Darya River. The two boys in the story eventually came to live in North America and both still recall the trip as a strange influence on their lives. The complete story can be found in the *Mennonite Encyclopedia* under "Claas Epp."

UNMENDING WALLS

By A. Grace Wenger

THE JEEP was aged and ailing, and Ken had named it Adam because of its unmistakable antiquity. That was at first sight. Closer acquaintance with its moods had made him rechristen it Eve. Now, after two years of familiarity with its whims, he coaxed the coughing motor almost mechanically.

"Eve gives you very much trouble, doesn't she?"

Ken looked up into the laughing blue eyes of his German friend Hans. "Yeah, she often complains like this. I'll have her humming pretty soon, I hope."

"Her name is well chosen," Hans commented, lingering as though he had something more significant to say.

"Say, what's got into the girls this morning?" Ken asked suddenly. "Do you have any idea?"

Hans became cautious. "Well, I don't know exactly. Girls have strange ideas sometimes. It seems now as though — somehow — they have taken a dislike to the new girl, the American."

"Not Phyllis!"

"Yes, that's the one."

Ken's eyes followed Phyllis as she walked up the path and disappeared around the corner of the barracks. Somehow she seemed different from the half-frightened girl who had arrived at the camp in a rickety Austrian taxi late last night. This morning she was poised and lovely and just a bit aloof. In the filmy green print that made her look as though she had stepped from the page of an American women's magazine, she seemed strangely out of place. The others were wearing old skirts or shabby jeans as if announcing to anyone interested that they had come to the international student work camp really to work. Ken felt troubled. Last night he had thought extravagantly that Phyllis was just the person to make the camp complete. This morning she seemed like a misfit.

"Christa says," Hans continued, "that she's either a millionaire or trying to make us think she is one, dressing like that to handle a shovel and hoe."

So that's what Christa had been excited about at breakfast. Ken had realized then that something was wrong. The work camp atmosphere of hearty cheer was falling flat. He had tried small talk with Christa, who sat beside him; but, instead of the cheerful banter he had expected in reply, she had answered politely in her best English. Then she turned to Hans and began to speak in German, so rapidly and low that Ken could not translate.

Hans was warming up to his subject now. "Christa says she has face cream and sunburn lotions enough to stock a shop. And this morning she took the basin out to the pump and scrubbed it before she washed her face. 'Just as though we were all diseased,' Christa says."

Eve's motor chose that moment to burst into a steady roar. Ken switched off the ignition impatiently.

"Look here, Hans," he said evenly. "You know as well as I do that she's not trying to act like a millionaire. That's an ordinary dress. It's pretty, sure, but not expensive. Maybe it's not exactly appropriate for work camp, but this is Phyllis' first experience at this sort of thing. How was she to know what kind of outfit to bring?"

Hans raised his hand in mock defense.

"One moment, my friend," he laughed. "I am not criticizing the American girl. I am only quoting Christa. You asked to know the cause of trouble, remember?"

"Yes, I know. But can't you help Christa and the others see that Phyllis is really all right. She's new and probably scared of the rest of you. Why not make a special effort to be friendly with her? Try drawing her into your group. She'll thaw out, I'm sure."

Hans grinned. "Wouldn't it be better if you championed the young lady's cause yourself?"

Ken turned on the ignition and resumed his struggle with Eve. "Eve and I are canvassing the countryside for potatoes this morning," he explained. "At the rate you boys tore into them this morning, we'll need a carload every day. I'm sure Erik ate ten pounds. And you weren't far behind."

"Then you won't be working on the job this morning?"

"Not until around nine o'clock, perhaps later. By the time I get there you'll have all the girls jollied into good spirits again."

Hans seemed dubious. "I'll see what I can do," he

promised. "I know the success of the camp is important to you," he said as he turned to leave.

"Thanks. I'm sure you can do it."

Ken watched as his friend headed for the barracks. Hans was right. This camp was important to him, and it was fellows like Hans and Erik who made him realize its importance. The three of them had met just about a year ago at a work camp similar to this one. Erik and Hans had been cool at first, with each other and with Ken. Dutch and German could not quite forget the old hatreds, and both were suspicious of the American. The reserve had broken down so gradually that Ken was hardly aware of what was happening until one day he realized that they were exchanging memories of wartime experiences, calmly and without blame. Ken had not forgotten how Hans had said, "Here is the worth of a camp like this — that one can learn to know as persons those he considered enemies."

As Eve coughed and roared into action, Ken thought ruefully that, during his two years of voluntary relief service in Europe, he had spent far more time nursing Eve's ailments than he had in building international understanding. It was only fair, of course, that the fellows with college training and all that should have the important jobs, but sometimes being man-of-all-work had seemed pretty dull and insignificant. This was his first chance to lead a student work camp — his lucky break. If he succeeded he'd have more assignments like this in the work he really wanted to do. If he failed, he'd continue as truck driver and mechanic.

Last evening Ken had felt so sure of himself. They were off to a good start. Germans, Dutch, French, English, Italians, and himself (the only American) had sat long around the U-shaped table and talked and laughed, good-naturedly translating for those who didn't understand and being amused at the difficulty of explaining even the most simple ideas in other languages. And the sober-eyed little refugee boys and girls had stood outside the window of the schoolhouse, watching the merriment of the foreign young people who had come to help to build houses, until their mothers called from the doorways of the crude barracks that it was time to come home. Then Phyllis had come.

Even so Ken felt quite confident that a morning of working together would kill the germ of ill will, especially if Hans were in the group. It would be much better for camp spirit if it were Hans and not he who championed the cause of another American.

It was nearly ten before Ken headed Eve past the row of unfinished cinder block houses to the field where the campers were excavating. In the midmorning heat, work was lagging. Phyllis was leaning on her shovel, looking slightly wilted, but still pretty. Her cheeks, forehead, and nose were already red. That sunburn lotion wasn't mere luxury, Ken thought. Hans was working near her, stopping often to talk. Erik was sitting on the edge of the excavation, swinging his long legs, loudly and cheerfully denouncing the heat of the Austrian sun, the hardness of Austrian rock, and the lack of good machinery such as was to be found in Holland. The others were resting or working ever so slowly. Only Christa seemed to be the impersonation of energy. Her muscular arms moved in a vigorous rhythm, and each shovelful of earth and stone thumped into the wheelbarrow like an accusation to all who were neglecting plain duty. Ken picked up a spare shovel and joined her.

"If everyone worked like you, Christa," he began,

"by the end of the summer there wouldn't be a home-less refugee in all of Austria."

Christa jabbed her shovel in a heap of earth, wiped her hands on her faded denim skirt, and faced Ken.

"And if everyone worked no more than some people," she retorted, "there wouldn't be a single house built all summer."

Ken laughed uneasily. "Oh, sometimes it takes a few days for people to get into the swing of this kind of work."

"People who don't want to work should not come to work camp," Christa announced with finality. "That American girl has done nothing more strenuous than make eyes at Hans all morning." She picked up her shovel and said grimly, "Hans ought to know better than to give attention to such things."

"Perhaps if you girls were more friendly to the American girl, she'd pay less attention to Hans," Ken suggested.

"One can't be friendly with a person like that! She feels too superior to the rest of us."

"What makes you say that, Christa? Has she told you so?"

"Not in words, but in actions. It's the clothes she wears and the way she wears them. It's the way she looks at everything, as if examining it for dirt. It's not so much any one thing as that superior air about her. She wears canvas gloves to work and even offered a pair to me. And this morning she gave a chocolate bar to everyone in the camp."

"Was there anything wrong with that?" Ken asked.

"You Americans are all alike. You hand out gifts all around — and you can easily afford to give from your abundance. Then you think the whole world ought to bow before you in humble gratitude."

Ken was saved from the necessity of replying by the arrival of two refugee women with a midmorning snack.

"Hurrah! Second breakfast." Erik was already examining the contents of the basket. The others gathered with renewed energy. Ken forced himself to eat a sandwich of crusty brown bread thickly spread with lard. (He knew the refugee women thought they were offering a delicacy.) Ken managed to swallow the greasy bread with the help of huge gulps of bitter synthetic coffee. He saw Phyllis take one bite, gingerly open the sandwich and examine the filling. Then she thrust the rest of the bread down a crevice in the stack of lumber on which she was sitting. It was done quickly; but Ken, watching Christa, was certain that the action had not escaped her watchful eye.

Now Phyllis toyed with the tin cup and made a half-hearted pretense of drinking her coffee. Obviously she hadn't been prepared for the ruggedness of life here. She had probably come with the idea that summer in an international work camp would be an adventure. Was she really as critical as Christa thought, or was she unaware of the impression she was leaving? He'd have to have a frank talk with her. If he could make her understand how sensitive the others were and how careful one had to be to avoid offending them, everything might work out all right. Only he'd have to talk to her soon before any new trouble developed.

The refugee women started to pack up the tin cups and leftover sandwiches. Ken walked over to the nearer of the two. "Your kitchen work keeps you busy," he said in German.

"Yes." The patient eyes lighted. "This is a large family you have brought us."

"Perhaps you'd like to have one of the girls help you

each afternoon. We can spare one from the project quite easily."

"That would be a great help."

"How would you like an American helper today?"

"That will be interesting indeed."

"All right. I'll see what I can do." Ken's plan was forming rapidly. If Phyllis worked in the kitchen today, he would have a chance to talk to her there. The refugee women who served as cooks did not know enough English to follow a discussion. There would be no danger of interruptions from the other campers. They would work until four, and then head for the river to swim; Ken was sure of that. No one would want to come to the overheated little shack that served as camp kitchen.

Ken approached Phyllis where she sat on the stack of boards. The other campers were returning to work with cheerful chatter and clanging of shovels and pickaxes. But Phyllis seemed not to notice. Her brown eyes swept far over the shimmering landscape and rested wistfully on the clusters of green treetops that marked the course of the river. She seemed to be trying to forget the trampled grass, the stacks of cinder blocks, the heaps of sand and stone, and the other workers. Ken felt somewhat hesitant about approaching her. He couldn't quite imagine her paring potatoes or washing dishes. He had to force himself to see his plan through.

"Tired?" he began.

"All over," she nodded. "And blistered too." She held out her palms. They were painfully red with a huge blister at the base of each thumb.

"Ever use a shovel before?" he asked.

"I never touched one," she admitted. "Hereafter I shall feel a keen sympathy for all excavators and grave diggers and a profound respect for whoever invented the bull-dozer.''

"The cooks would like to have one of the girls help them in the kitchen each afternoon. How would you like to take your turn today?''

"Instead of shoveling these ghastly rocks! I'd be delighted.''

"It may mean giving up your free time later this afternoon. Are you sure it's all right?''

"Definitely. When do I begin?''

"Immediately after lunch. You'll probably have to wash dishes, and then help prepare dinner.''

She glanced at her watch — a tiny gold one, Ken noticed, probably another source of offense to Christa.

"One hour, thirty and one half more minutes with the shovel. You've saved the day for me.''

She jumped up and started toward the excavation. Ken followed.

"Of course, you understand it's not a model kitchen. I don't want you to be too badly disappointed when you see it.''

"I've already seen it. I peeked this morning. Couldn't resist it. I'm a home ec major, you see. I'm rather intrigued by the idea of trying to cook an edible meal in iron pots on a woodburning stove.''

She ran lightly down the board that served as a track for the wheelbarrow, picked up a shovel, and attacked the stony earth with jerky thrusts. Ken grinned.

"Seems to me a home ec curriculum ought to include at least one course in the proper handling of garden tools,'' he said as he walked past her to help Christa.

Although Christa wasn't inclined to talk, Ken as he swung his pickax with slow sure strokes, felt better than he had all day. Phyllis wasn't one bit snobbish after all. All she needed was a little help in sensing the situation. She'd be all right. If she'd just make more of an effort to be sociable, even Christa would come around all right, provided Phyllis weren't too friendly with Hans. He'd have to throw out a broad hint that Christa considered Hans fair game for only German girls. It was certainly true that Hans and Phyllis seemed to have found a great deal in common in a few hours' time. He saw them laughing and talking companionably as they worked together. Ken felt a touch of resentment and a slight kinship with Christa. He stole another look at the fiercely energetic German girl and decided that one o'clock couldn't come too soon. He wouldn't feel really at ease until lunch was over and Phyllis was safely established in the kitchen. She'd be safe enough there until he had a chance to talk to her; and after that, well, he realized he was staking a good deal on his faith in her common sense.

AT FOUR o'clock, after he had seen the others start across the meadow to the river, Ken headed for the kitchen. An excited Frau Schurz met him at the doorway.

"The bread! It is not here," she moaned to Ken.

"What's the matter? Haven't you enough for supper?"

"For the evening meal, yes. But not for breakfast. The baker promised to send his boy with it. I think he has forgotten. We have not the time to go for it this afternoon. And this evening the shop will be closed."

"It wouldn't be possible to plan a breadless breakfast?" Ken suggested.

"Ach, no. Those who work must have bread to eat." Frau Schurz uttered the words with the air of one proclaiming a timeless truth.

"I'll take the jeep and get it for you right now," Ken offered. In a matter of minutes he knew he could drive the few miles to the little bakery and back.

But after Ken had set the baskets of huge round loaves in the jeep and had listened patiently to the lengthy apologies of the forgetful baker, he found Eve more stubborn than usual. She coughed and sputtered in her usual way and then died down with the whine that always heralded serious trouble. Ken tinkered with the ailing engine impatiently, but it was nearly two hours before he finally arrived back in camp. The little cluster of campers around the community pump was evidence that the others had returned from their swim. The kitchen was empty. Apparently the cooks had already carried the food to the dining room. His chance for a private talk with Phyllis was gone.

He set the bread baskets on the kitchen table and started toward the pump. As he approached he heard Erik's loud tenor, "There will be potatoes, I hope, and plenty of them." Ken found himself hoping, more for Phyllis's sake than for Erik's, that Phyllis hadn't persuaded the cooks to let her try out any American dishes.

However, the minute he stepped into the empty schoolroom that served as combination dining room and lounge, Ken realized that was just what had happened. The entire meal was strictly American. Huge individual salads looked strangely foreign on the battered enamel plates. There were dainty sandwiches; the bread looked paper thin compared to the slabs the refugee women served. Two huge chocolate cakes adorned the tables, and closer inspection revealed cold tea in the tin cups, not hot. (It couldn't be iced, for there wasn't any ice to be had.)

Anyone who could rustle up a meal like that in the

camp kitchen with camp provisions was really an accomplished cook. But Ken had misgivings. This radical departure from work camp cookery was not going to increase Phyllis's popularity. She was filling the last cups with tea, innocent as could be, looking so pleased that it hurt. The others were finding their places silently, exchanging dubious glances.

They were good enough sports at first. A French girl said politely, "It is an American custom, is it not, to serve tea cold?" After her first taste, Christa gave her salad plate a little shove and said softly to Hans, "Sweet and sour together. This is not fit to eat." But Erik, after consuming two sandwiches in as many bites, looked around in mock wonder, grinned boyishly, and demanded, "And when is the *food* coming?"

Amid the general laughter Christa's voice could be heard saying quite clearly to Hans, "Not only must we take orders from an American leader; we must also eat American food."

Ken was vaguely aware of Hans' troubled expression. He was seeing above all else the hurt look on Phyllis's face. He felt helpless, absolutely helpless, and annoyed with himself. It was stupid to have used Phyllis in the kitchen the first day. He might have foreseen that something like this would happen.

Erik rushed out of the room. No one knew why, until he returned several minutes later with two loaves of the newly baked bread, a good-sized wedge of cheese, and a huge carving knife. He dumped the bread and cheese on the table and handed the knife to Christa.

"I have found food," he announced. "Here, Christa, cut it so that a person has something to sink his teeth into."

Even those who had been too polite to protest openly

ate huge chunks of bread and cheese with gusto, leaving the salads barely touched.

Ken, watching Phyllis as she toyed with her own salad, saw the flush on her cheeks deepen. Her eyes weren't hurt now; they were angry. He didn't exactly blame her, only he hoped she wouldn't explode. But she did.

"Well, of all the nerve!" she exclaimed sharply. "Here I've been slaving in that hot shack of a kitchen while the rest of you went swimming. You might show a bit of gratitude even if it's not the food you're used to."

She got up as if to leave the room. But she turned back again. Her voice became scornful. "I thought you might like a change from the everlasting bread and cheese and meat and potatoes I've seen on every single table — breakfast, dinner, and supper — ever since I arrived in Austria. But of course you don't want that. You'll go on eating bread and cheese and meat and potatoes till doomsday like your fathers and grandfathers and great-grandfathers did before you. You're too stubborn to change. I believe you're scared of any change."

Ken was at her side now. "Please stop it, Phyllis." His quiet entreaty was more like a command.

Phyllis turned on him. She spoke dramatically, loudly, for all to hear. "Hasn't it occurred to you that you're wasting your time here? These people don't want to learn new ways of doing things. They're snobs. They love their barriers and dislike strangers. No wonder Europe's always having war. No wonder — "

Ken could think of only one way to stop her. He grabbed her by the shoulders and shook her roughly.

Phyllis burst into tears.

Ken said as calmly as he could, "Hans, you will take charge of the evening program." Then he took Phyllis firmly by the arm and marched her into the warm July twilight. The silence he left behind him felt brittle, like an icicle. "International understanding," he mocked silently. "It's more like a kids' party game — a pantomime of the cold war."

But it was civil war he had to reckon with now. His countrywoman jerked her arm away and faced him.

"And you — you're worse than any of them," she sobbed. "Tactics of a Nazi general!"

"Okay. So we're exchanging compliments." Ken spoke with the bitterness of a man who has watched a cherished dream shatter. "I think you've just put on the most revolting act I've ever seen. Spoiled baby having a temper tantrum!"

She stalked away without answering.

Going to her cot to finish her cry, Ken decided.

But she swept around the corner and out of sight.

As far as I'm concerned she can walk clear to Linz, catch the next train for Paris, and fly home, he thought.

Not that her going would help the situation now. It was beyond remedy. He could make polite apologies and explanations, but words would not heal the hurt that had been inflicted. Nothing that could be said now would restore the comradely give-and-take atmosphere that was so necessary. He was a failure as a leader.

Ken stood there in the darkness for what seemed like a long time. Then he patted Eve's battered fender. "Looks like you and I'll be buddies for a long, long time, old girl," he told her.

Suddenly he started down the path. If Phyllis had gone to the kitchen in that mood she'd insult every cook in the place. He'd end up as camp chef.

However, as he approached the camp kitchen, he was

surprised to hear women's voices singing, of all things, "Silent Night," in German. He was even more surprised when he entered. The cooks were hurrying about, singing as they worked. And there was Phyllis, kneeling on the floor, washing dishes in a huge tub, singing along with them. A smudge of soot streaked her face and her offensive dress was almost completely concealed under the shapeless black apron that Frau Schurz usually wore. But her voice was sweeter than he dreamed it could be as she finished the stanza, "*Schlaf in himmlicher Ruhe.*"

"It's the only German song I know," she explained when she saw him. "Not too inappropriate at that, is it?" she added, half mischievously.

Then she stood up and her eyes were serious. "How does one apologize in acceptable European fashion? Especially if one speaks only American English?" she asked.

Before Ken could answer, she went on. "You're quite right. I am a spoiled baby. Only most people don't have the nerve to tell me in so many words. It did hurt — really."

Ken hesitated. He wasn't quite convinced that she was sincere.

"Yes, I know I was hateful," she admitted. "And I know how to apologize to you. But the others — what shall I say to them?"

Ken spoke slowly. "Perhaps you'd better say nothing. Seems to me that's something you'll have to live down rather than talk about. Being friendly and considerate, if you really mean it, will be a better apology than any words you can say."

"I do mean it." She turned toward him and the brown eyes that met his were serious. Then she wiped her hands nervously on the clumsy black apron. "But can I make them believe I do — after the crazy way I blew my top today?"

Ken couldn't make himself hate her now. He forced himself to answer cheerfully. "Sure, you can. You've got six whole weeks to undo the work of a day. Of course you can do it." He held out his hand. "Let's go back together and begin now."

"Not yet." She turned back determinedly to the stack of unwashed enamel plates. "I've a job to finish here. Besides," she hesitated, "I'm not sure I have the courage to face them tonight."

Ken didn't like facing those hostile eyes any better than she did, but it wouldn't be any easier tomorrow. As he walked toward the schoolhouse, he felt a sudden sympathy for war criminals.

But when he entered the room and stood before his international court, the glances that met his were more curious than unfriendly.

Hans was the first to speak. "Quick, tell us, how did it turn out?" he demanded. "Erik and Christa are becoming Americanized. They have wagered their chocolate bars on the outcome. Who won?"

Ken answered at once. "She owns she's been a heel — she admits that her conduct was unpleasant," he remembered to interpret. "She asks, not for immediate pardon, but for a chance to prove that she really wants to be a friend."

Erik cheered. "I knew you'd do it. When you marched her out of this room, I knew you'd win."

Christa curtsied elaborately and handed a candy bar to Erik. "The chocolate is yours," she said.

Then she turned to Ken. "Tell me one thing more," she said soberly, but her twinkling eyes betrayed her.

"Where did you learn so well how to handle an emotional woman?"

Ken's laugh was contagious. "Well, you know," he returned her mock serious approach, "I've had two years of experience with Eve — the most unpredictable of them all."

FROM ACROSS THE TRACKS

By Merle Good

"IS THE CATHODE negative?" That was all the note said. It was scribbled on the back of a dirty index card. Tony wouldn't have noticed it if he hadn't looked up to see how much time he had to finish the chemistry test. The quarterback across the aisle had propped the card against the seat in front of him, turning it toward Tony.

Tony didn't move. He stared at his test sheet. Two short minutes of test time remained. He had three problems to complete. And they were tough ones. He wanted to concentrate.

But his mind was in a whirl. He couldn't think. All that flashed on his mental screen was: *Is the cathode negative?* He knew the answer. And a nod of his head would relay the information to the quarterback.

But was it right? True, the big fellow was popular. He belonged to one of those more wealthy Negro families that had moved into those new houses on Market Street. And he could play football well enough, too. The students called him Sneaky because of his perfection of the quarterback sneak.

But Sneaky often boasted of not needing to study. So why help him cheat? Maybe this would show him he's not the big cheese, after all.

A glance at the clock showed one minute remaining. Out of the corner of his eye, Tony saw Nancy Miller's pretty red head nodding to Sneaky. Nancy sat on the other side of the quarterback, opposite Tony. She was one of the cheerleaders for the squad.

Then the bell rang. Mr. Nonstone came from the lab to collect the test papers. Tony handed his sheet to the teacher and headed down the hall for the locker room. School was over for the day and he wanted to pick up his gym bag before heading home.

He lived about a mile out of town — across the tracks. He had two sisters and a kid brother. Folks seldom saw his mother; they said she was sickly. And they said something about his pap dying in a train crash several years back.

The guys called him Tony only in class. Otherwise, any of a score of uncomplimentary nicknames did the job. He worked evenings on a neighbor's farm. He walked to work, and to school, too. His family had no car.

But Tony was intelligent. He liked school, especially chemistry. Teachers said he should go to college. He knew better. Work comes first. In fact, that's why he didn't try out for the football team in August. His family needed him.

Tony flicked the dial of his lock, roughly, three times and it dropped open. He was still provoked. Sneaky thought he was hot stuff. That's the way some of those Negroes were. Oh, lots of Negroes were good people. So were a good many whites. But there were bad ones in every crowd. And some of those people down on Market Street thought they owned the civil rights bill. Take Sneaky's dad, for instance — he was always out front demonstrating, fighting for more freedom, and talking big.

Tony reached for his gym bag. As he slipped the lock back on, he heard someone behind him. Swinging around he found Sneaky standing over him. *Must have followed me,* Tony thought.

"Okay, you squirrel," the quarterback chewed the words. "You'll pay for that one."

Tony barely saw the punch before it hit his cheek. He leaped to his feet, lifting clenched fists to strike back. But conscience delayed his reaction. For a moment, he saw his mother's tired face. She often begged him not to fight. Too much hatred in the world as it is, she said.

But Tony forgot his mother when the quarterback's fist came back, smashing against his forehead. Tony caught his balance, bracing himself against the lockers. Then, with blinding speed, he hooked the big boy on the jaw with a solid jab. With a curse, Sneaky slumped to the bench.

Tony left by the back corridor. He usually did. He would not meet as many people that way. Nor would he have to walk as far. One mile was far enough.

He saw the redheaded cheerleader coming from the science wing. He decided to take the south walk to avoid her. Nancy was cute enough. But she was one of the gang. They were all the same — proud, deceptive, two-faced.

"Tony."

He kept on walking. What would she want with him? Must be another gimmick to bug him. He was in no mood for more tricks.

"Tony."

She was closer. She must be running. *But what's the score? Who's she trying to fool?*

He stopped when she called a third time. She was more gorgeous than he remembered as she came running toward him, her short skirt flitting about long legs, hair streaming and eyes bright as the breeze pressed her sweater softly against small breasts.

"Tony, you can play football, can't you?" Her tone was at once both sensuous and earnest.

For a moment, his heart melted. Football had always been his favorite sport. He remembered how his dad had often played with him when they used to pick tomatoes with the migrants. They lived in the farmer's brooder house, and the meadow nearby suited their football purposes well. But what was Nancy up to now?

"Our Sunday school class is having a social next Saturday afternoon. We are going to play football just for fun. And each of us is to try to bring someone new."

Tony puzzled. Sunday school? So Nancy was religious. He could have known. He should have known, really. That's the way these church people were.

He remembered how his mother used to take him to church when they had lived with the migrants. But his father had never gone with them.

"My boy, there are two words I have learned to hate," he had told Tony, "the one is 'rich' and the other is 'church.'" Tony could still see the look of disgust on his face. It was one of the last things he recalled his dad saying before the train mishap.

"Tony," he used to say, "for seven summers, I worked for a man who called himself a Christian. He would invite me to church, sometimes. Mennonite. But I knew darn well all that man wanted was my cheap labor, and nothing else mattered. And if that's what it means to be a Christian — well, son, the less you have to do with it, the better."

Nancy waited, almost nervously.

Tony remained silent.

So Nancy tried to explain. "Our pastor says we should get out and witness more to people. And so our class thought . . ." Her voice trailed off as she hesitated, her lips forming a small nervous smile.

Tony was angry. So she was out to help sinners, was she? And just who were the sinners? What about Sneaky? If she could help him cheat, she could try to make him religious, too. It might do him some good. And maybe she could invite herself while she was at it.

Tony's eyes lighted, then narrowed. His face tensed. He stepped toward Nancy, extending his hand. His whisper was barely audible, cold with resentment. "This is not 'Be kind to Puerto Rican Week,'" he said bitterly. And then he slapped her.

A moment later, he was gone.

A VISIT TO THE ZOO

By Levi Miller

IT WAS ONLY ten o'clock in the morning, but the sky was clear and the sun was hot, so hot that the mother was carrying her shawl folded over her arms which she locked together in front of her. In her hand she carried a white handkerchief with a pink crocheted border. She wiped her forehead with it.

As she looked across the asphalt sidewalks that formed a network all over the sprawling Cleveland zoo grounds she could see the blackness dissolve into a mirage on the smooth surface. Occasionally a peacock would interrupt the hum of the zoo with his shrill cry. The air seemed weighted with a subdued smell of animal manure.

The father had taken off his coat. He was wearing a blue, long-sleeved shirt and a black vest that matched his trousers. He had rolled up the shirt sleeves exactly one time.

Three little girls giggled as they licked their snow cones, all a bright cherry color, and stayed close to their mother.

The little boy walked by his father's side. In his hands he tightly grasped a big bag. His black hat was tilted back so that the light breeze would cool his forehead. At other times he would take it off and fan his face. He was talking to his father.

"What was the man doing at the gate?"

"He was collecting money."

"Is that all he does?"

"Yes." The father said it absentmindedly. They were talking in Pennsylvania German, their native language.

"Then why didn't he let us carry the peanut bag in right away?"

"He didn't know us."

"Didn't he trust us?"

"He didn't know us."

"But he wouldn't have had to pour them all out and call in those other men. Such a fuss." He paused and tossed the peanut bag on top of his shoulders. The father seemed not to hear and the boy's mind was moving rapidly. "Will they feed the animals while we're here? I'd like to see that."

They kept on walking together. They were going to see the elephants. They had decided that morning on the way to the zoo that they would first visit the elephants and then the monkeys. The car driver, who was now dozing in the front seat of the car, had said that the best thing to see was the penguins; the father had wanted to go to the big cats; but the mother and the four children had decided to see the elephants and monkeys first.

This was the first visit of the family to the zoo. The father and mother had gone to the zoo when they were children and during their teen years before marriage, but they never got a chance to take their children after they were married. They were too busy on the 80-acre farm they had bought. For the past several summers they had said they were going to visit the zoo but they never went. Always hay was lying, a cow was sick, or corn needed to be husked.

As they came to the elephant yards the pungent manure smell became stronger. A bull elephant was in a small yard beyond a six-foot-wide concrete dry moat that separated him from the people. On the outside of the moat was a low wall of about three feet. A chain followed the bull as he walked back and forth. First he would walk in one direction until he almost came to the end of his chain and then he would stop. He seemed to know exactly how long the chain was because he never jerked it taut; he would stop just before it tightened. Then he would turn around, throw his trunk up and go back in the other direction. As he walked his trunk always swung back and forth, always swinging. A smaller elephant was on the one side of him. This one, a female, was also walking back and forth.

"Isn't he big!" It was one of the little girls talking about the bull elephant.

"He's so lonely."

"They use them in India to pull logs."

"Wouldn't they be strong to plow?" the boy said to the father as he leaned over the low wall.

"I wish they'd let him loose."

"Why don't they let them together?"

"It wouldn't work." The father answered the little girl

without looking at her. He was looking only at the bull elephant.

"Remember the story our teacher told us about the blind men and the elephant . . . hee, he, hee . . ."

"Don't talk silly." The mother had never heard the story.

"Look, *da Dat* is talking to him." That's what they called the father, *da Dat*.

"*Da Dat* knows elephant language." They were laughing.

"He's slowing down. The elephant is listening to *da Dat*. Throw him some peanuts, *Dat!*"

But the father didn't throw him any peanuts. He just chewed some himself and looked directly at the bull elephant. The little boy held the big bag of peanuts up to his father — the bag of peanuts that had caused the long delay at the gate. The official said he could not have people bringing big bags of peanuts for the animals. How do they know there was not poison in them or something to make the animals sick?

"I grew them." The father had said. "They come from my farm."

"But how do we know they are good?"

"Nobody else had them. I had them in my house and stored there in sacks."

The little boy remembered how he had helped his father to harvest them in the fall and sack them and how they had talked about bringing some to the zoo the next summer. But three summers and three winters in which they saved peanuts went by and they never visited the zoo, not until now.

The elephant stopped completely. He was looking right at the father and the father was still talking to him in a soft and even voice. The bull elephant's eyes blinked slowly and some flies buzzed around his ears, but he hardly flapped them. He was looking only at the father.

"Throw him some peanuts!" the little boy said in Pennsylvania German.

"Elephants know their language," an onlooker remarked. "Isn't that something?"

"Maybe it's because they're like the animals, so close to them," another suggested.

"Oh, stop it. Quit being so condescending."

"Ah, they'll do it for anyone."

"Look at the little ones," someone said, nodding toward the children.

"They don't even understand us. Do they talk English?"

"You can throw them some peanuts, ah, ah, Mis . . ., Sir, Mister."

A crowd had gathered and people were talking and watching. The family was huddled together directly in front of the elephant. The mother was looking down at her feet. She nervously took the black shawl, unfolded it, and threw it over her shoulders even though it was hot. You could see the little white A.Y. initials in one corner as she unfolded it. The A.Y. stood for Anna Yoder. She held two of the girls' hands. They looked up and she looked down. The crowd got larger and people came closer.

The little boy was unaware of the people as he watched his father. He didn't say a word as the father kept talking to the elephant in unintelligible guttural sounds. Then slowly he put his hand down into the peanut bag that the boy was holding and took out a peanut and cracked the shell. He threw the shell into the moat and rubbed off the thin skin. The elephant had come up to the moat as far as his chain would let him. He knew when he was the full length of the chain because he stopped just before it pulled taut. As he stood and listened to the father, his trunk extended far out like the arm of a small crane. The father threw the peanut high, arching it into the sky. The little yellow nut glistened in the sun and the elephant moved his arm just slightly and the peanut was in the scoop.

"Do it again!"

"Give me some peanuts. I want to feed him too."

Someone threw a peanut at the entranced animal but the elephant did not move. The peanut rolled off his side and on to the ground.

"Look at the little girls. Aren't they cute. They're so bashful."

"Sally, bring me that bloody camera!"

"He's talking to him again."

"Tell them to go away," the boy said to the father.

"They want to see the elephant."

"No." The boy whispered to the father even if no one could understand but the family. "They want to see you — and us! They don't care about the elephant. Why don't they leave us alone?"

The father didn't say any more to the boy. Again he talked to the elephant. He took out another peanut. Again he threw it high across the moat that separated the elephant from the people. Just as it reached its arch several cameras clicked in rapid fire.

"I got him, Sally. Just as he was throwing it."

"Ah, Mister, Sir, excuse me. I'm Mr. Johnson from the *Cleveland Daily News*. Could I have your name, please?"

The father abruptly took the son's hand and turned around. He picked up the smallest girl and threw her over his shoulder where she buried her face in the hairy opening between the brim of his hat and his shoulder. He didn't look around, or up, only down.

"*Kom, mom, de Leut sind net chat,*" he said in German to the mother. (Come, Mother, the people are crazy.)

"Sir, I'd only like to have your name for this photo in the *Daily News*. That's all . . . and where you're from."

He received no answer.

"First time to the zoo? You sure know how to handle elephants."

The father was walking toward the monkey island and he did not say anything. The mother followed with the other two girls still hanging onto her shawl and hands. The peacocks screamed on the lawn. Over on a hillside you could see mountain goats standing perfectly motionless in what was supposed to be a natural setting.

"Buy your peanuts here!" called a vendor on the grass just off the sidewalk. "Feed the animals peanuts."

The family did not look up at him. They could now see the monkey island, an elevated heap of rock and soil. Up on top there was a big spoked wheel which the monkeys were turning.

"Hee, he, hee. Look at them, *Dat.*"

"Where are we going after we see the monkeys? I want another ice-cream cone." She really meant a red cherry snow cone but it was all the same to her.

The reporter came running and the little girls again ducked their heads into the mother's shawl. He was panting and flushed as he tapped the father on the shoulder. "I'm sorry, sir, I was offensive. I didn't know you didn't want to have your picture taken. My apologies to all of you."

"Ah, that's okay."

"You did so well with that elephant."

"Naw."

"Can you do that with other animals?"

"Ya."

"May I watch you?"

"Naw, I'd rather you wouldn't."

"Well, sir, if I could only have your names."

"*Sag ihm far veck gehe.*" The little girl whispered into her father's ear. (Tell him to go away.)

There was a long silence and then a monkey screeched and the old spoked wheel began turning. The family looked around and the reporter walked away. The sun shone almost directly overhead now and the little boy shaded his eyes with his hat as he looked up into his father's face.

"*Dat,* where did you learn to talk to elephants?"

"I used to work at a circus."

"When? Where?!" The little girl peeked out from her shelter in her father's neck.

"Before we were married. I ran away for a winter and worked at the Ringling Brothers Circus for one winter in Florida."

"Why didn't you ever tell me?" The boy's voice was strained but eager. His eyes were fixed on his father.

"You shouldn't tell him things like that," said the mother, taking off her shawl again and carefully folding it.

The family walked up to the fence surrounding the water that was around the monkey island and watched the monkeys play and spin on the old wooden wheel with spokes.

THE AUTHORS

Good, Merle. Merle and his wife, Phyllis, now live and teach at Lancaster Mennonite High School, from which he graduated in 1964. They also serve as producers of the Dutch Family Festival in Lancaster, Pennsylvania, each summer. He has authored two other books, four musicals, and four plays. His novel *Happy as the Grass Was Green* has been filmed as a major motion picture.

Hoover, Sharon. Sharon wrote "Waiting" as a seventeen-year-old senior at Lancaster Mennonite High School. Her home is in Leola, Pennsylvania. She says, "I'm still in the midst of wondering if writing is a hobby or a chore for me. Writing aside, I enjoy acting and singing (for my own pleasure) and simply interacting with people."

Leatherman, Lois. Lois is a 1972 graduate of Eastern Mennonite College, Harrisonburg, Virginia, with a BA in music and English. She spent a year in Germany under the auspices of the University of Oregon's German Music Center. Presently employed by Provident Bookstore, Lancaster, Pennsylvania, she is continuing private music studies.

Lehman, Melvin. Melvin grew up in Lancaster County, Pennsylvania. Following graduation in 1971 from Eastern Mennonite College, Harrisonburg, Virginia, he drove a taxi in Washington, D.C. He has contributed various short stories and articles to Mennonite publications. "The Tent" first appeared in *Christian Living* in 1969 and "The Departure" in 1972.

Miller, Levi. Levi is an editor in the Congregational Literature Division of Mennonite Publishing House, Scottdale, Pennsylvania. Currently a member of Mennonite Historical Committee and Thoreau Lyceum, he taught English in the public schools of Puerto Rico for two years. Levi and his wife, Gloria, are the parents of Jakob Levi. He attended Kent State and Malone College. A native of Holmes County, Ohio, most of his relatives are members of the Old Order Amish.

Reed, Kenneth. Ken describes himself as "a child of God of the Mennonite *Freundschaft,* a little over six feet, age 29, graduated from Lancaster Mennonite High and Eastern Mennonite College, formerly an English teacher in Asahikawa, Japan, and an editor for Mennonite Publishing House, childless, unmarried, and a tax-paying resident of Paradise, Pennsylvania." He is the author of a novel, *Mennonite Soldier*.

Smith, Eleanor. Eleanor, one of five children, grew up in Illinois and Kansas. She graduated from Goshen College, Goshen, Indiana, in 1965 and wrote "Sunday School" during her student days. She taught school for five years — first secondary, then elementary (in Puerto Rico), and finally college. In 1972 she quit teaching. "I began exploring community living and other interests rising to the top of my consciousness," she explains. "I hope to continue in community living, and possibly write and do office work for a small magazine that's trying to voice neglected questions and answers about peace, human kinship, and liberation."

Stahl, J. D. J. D. grew up in Luxembourg and Germany, the son of Mennonite missionaries. A graduate of Lancaster Mennonite High School and Goshen College (BA in English and German, 1973), he has taught high school English for a year, has had a number of articles, poems, and short stories appear in Mennonite periodicals, and intends to do graduate work in English.

Wenger, A. Grace. A. Grace lives in Leola, Pennsylvania. She received her BS degree from Elizabethtown College and her MA from the University of Pennsylvania. She has taught English in the Pennsylvania public schools and at Eastern Mennonite High School, Lancaster Mennonite High School, and Millersville State College. She is a member of the Mennonite Board of Education and a trustee of Eastern Mennonite College. She has written Herald Press curriculum and mission study books. She is an officer of Menno-Housing, Inc., and Tabor Community Services, equal opportunity and nonprofit housing organizations.